Ernest Miller Hemingway was born in 1899. His father was a doctor and he was the second of six children. Their home was at Oak Park, a Chicago suburb.

In 1917 Hemingway joined the Kansas City *Star* as a cub reporter. The following year he volunteered to work as an ambulance driver on the Italian front where he was badly wounded but twice decorated for his services. He returned to America in 1919 and married in 1921. In 1922 he reported on the Greco-Turkish war, then two years later resigned from journalism to devote himself to fiction. He settled in Paris where he renewed his earlier friendship with such fellow-American expatriates as Ezra Pound and Gertrude Stein. Their encouragement and criticism were to play a valuable part in the formation of his style.

Hemingway's first two published works were *Three Stories and Ten Poems* and *In Our Time*, but it was the satirical novel, *The Torrents of Spring*, which established his name more widely. His international reputation was firmly secured by his next three books: *Fiesta*, *Men Without Women* and *A Farewell to Arms*.

He was passionately involved with bullfighting, big-game hunting and deep-sea fishing, and his writing reflected this. He visited Spain during the Civil War and described his experiences in the bestseller, *For Whom the Bell Tolls*.

His direct and deceptively simple style of writing spawned generations of imitators but no equals. Recognition of his position in contemporary literature came in 1954 when he was awarded the Nobel Prize, following the publication of *The Old Man and the Sea*.

Ernest Hemingway died in 1961.

By the same author

Novels

The Torrents of Spring
Fiesta
A Farewell to Arms
To Have and Have Not
For Whom the Bell Tolls
Across the River and Into the Trees
The Old Man and the Sea
Islands in the Stream
The Garden of Eden

Stories

Winner Take Nothing
The Snows of Kilimanjaro

General

Death in the Afternoon
Green Hills of Africa
A Moveable Feast
The Dangerous Summer

Drama

The Fifth Column

Collected Works

The Essential Hemingway
The First Forty-Nine Stories
By-Line

ERNEST HEMINGWAY

Men Without Women

TriadGrafton
An Imprint of HarperCollins*Publishers*

Grafton
An Imprint of HarperCollins*Publishers*
77–85 Fulham Palace Road,
Hammersmith, London W6 8JB

Published by Grafton 1977
Reprinted nine times
9 8 7 6 5 4 3 2 1

First published in Great Britain by
Jonathan Cape Ltd 1928

ISBN 0 586 04472 8

Set in Garamond

Printed in Great Britain by
HarperCollinsManufacturing Glasgow

To
EVAN SHIPMAN

CONTENTS

THE UNDEFEATED

Manuel Garcia climbed the stairs to Don Miguel Retana's office. He set down his suitcase and knocked on the door. There was no answer. Manuel, standing in the hallway, felt there was someone in the room. He felt it through the door.

'Retana,' he said, listening.

There was no answer.

He's there, all right, Manuel thought.

'Retana,' he said and banged the door.

'Who's there?' said someone in the office.

'Me, Manolo,' Manuel said.

'What do you want?' asked the voice.

'I want to work,' Manuel said.

Something in the door clicked several times and it swung open. Manuel went in, carrying his suitcase.

A little man sat behind a desk at the far side of the room. Over his head was a bull's head, stuffed by a Madrid taxidermist; on the walls were framed photographs and bullfight posters.

The little man sat looking at Manuel.

'I thought they'd killed you,' he said.

Manuel knocked with his knuckles on the desk. The little man sat looking at him across the desk.

'How many corridas you had this year?' Retana asked.

'One,' he answered.

'Just that one?' the little man asked.

'That's all.'

'I read about it in the papers,' Retana said. He leaned back in the chair and looked at Manuel.

Manuel looked up at the stuffed bull. He had seen it often before. He felt a certain family interest in it. It had killed his brother, the promising one, about nine years ago. Manuel remembered the day. There was a brass plate on the oak shield the bull's head was mounted on. Manuel could not read it, but he imagined it was in memory of his brother. Well, he had been a good kid.

The plate said: 'The Bull "Mariposa" of the Duke of Veragua, which accepted 9 varas for 7 caballos, and caused the death of Antonio Garcia, Novillero, April 27, 1909.'

Retana saw him looking at the stuffed bull's head.

'The lot the Duke sent me for Sunday will make a scandal,' he said. 'They're all bad in the legs. What do they say about them at the Café?'

'I don't know,' Manuel said. 'I just got in.'

'Yes,' Retana said. 'You still have your bag.'

He looked at Manuel, leaning back behind the big desk.

'Sit down,' he said. 'Take off your cap.'

Manuel sat down; his cap off, his face was changed. He looked pale, and his coleta pinned forwards on his head, so that it would not show under the cap, gave him a strange look.

'You don't look well,' Retana said.

'I just got out of the hospital,' Manuel said.

'I heard they'd cut your leg off,' Retana said.

'No,' said Manuel. 'It got all right.'

Retana leaned forwards across the desk and pushed a wooden box of cigarettes towards Manuel.

'Have a cigarette,' he said.

'Thanks.'

Manuel lit it.

'Smoke?' he said, offering the match to Retana.

'No,' Retana waved his hand. 'I never smoke.'

Retana watched him smoking.

'Why don't you get a job and go to work?' he said.

'I don't want to work,' Manuel said. 'I am a bullfighter.'

'There aren't any bullfighters any more,' Retana said.

'I'm a bullfighter,' Manuel said.

'Yes, while you're in there,' Retana said.

Manuel laughed.

Retana sat, saying nothing and looking at Manuel.

'I'll put you in a nocturnal if you want,' Retana offered.

'When?' Manuel asked.

'Tomorrow night.'

'I don't like to substitute for anybody,' Manuel said. That

was the way they all got killed. That was the way Salvador got killed. He tapped with his knuckles on the table.

'It's all I've got,' Retana said.

'Why don't you put me on next week?' Manuel suggested.

'You wouldn't draw,' Retana said. 'All they want is Litri and Rubito and La Torre. Those kids are good.'

'They'd come to see me get it,' Manuel said, hopefully.

'No, they wouldn't. They don't know who you are any more.'

'I've got a lot of stuff,' Manuel said.

'I'm offering to put you on tomorrow night,' Retana said. 'You can work with young Hernandez and kill two novillos after the Charlots.'

'Whose novillos?' Manuel asked.

'I don't know. Whatever stuff they've got in the corrals. What the veterinaries won't pass in the daytime.'

'I don't like to substitute,' Manuel said.

'You can take it or leave it,' Retana said. He leaned forwards over the papers. He was no longer interested. The appeal that Manuel had made to him for a moment when he thought of the old days was gone. He would like to get him to substitute for Larita because he could get him cheaply. He could get others cheaply too. He would like to help him though. Still, he had given him the chance. It was up to him.

'How much do I get?' Manuel asked. He was still playing with the idea of refusing. But he knew he could not refuse.

'Two hundred and fifty pesetas,' Retana said. He had thought of five hundred, but when he opened his mouth it said two hundred and fifty.

'You pay Villalta seven thousand,' Manuel said.

'You're not Villalta,' Retana said.

'I know it,' Manuel said.

'He draws it, Manolo,' Retana said in explanation.

'Sure,' said Manuel. He stood up. 'Give me three hundred, Retana.'

'All right,' Retana agreed. He reached in the drawer for a paper.

'Can I have fifty now?' Manuel asked.

'Sure,' said Retana. He took a fifty peseta note out of his

pocket-book and laid it, spread out flat, on the table.

Manuel picked it up and put it in his pocket.

'What about a cuadrilla?' he asked.

'There's the boys that always work for me nights,' Retana said. 'They're all right.'

'How about picadors?' Manuel asked.

'They're not much,' Retana admitted.

'I've got to have one good pic,' Manuel said.

'Get him then,' Retana said. 'Go and get him.'

'Not out of this,' Manuel said. 'I'm not paying for any cuadrilla out of sixty duros.'

Retana said nothing but looked at Manuel across the big desk.

'You know I've got to have one good pic,' Manuel said.

Retana said nothing but looked at Manuel from a long way off.

'It isn't right,' Manuel said.

Retana was still considering him, leaning back in his chair, considering him from a long way away.

'There're the regular pics,' he offered.

'I know,' Manuel said. 'I know your regular pics.'

Retana did not smile. Manuel knew it was over.

'All I want is an even break,' Manuel said reasoningly. 'When I go out there I want to be able to call my shots on the bull. It only takes one good picador.'

He was talking to a man who was no longer listening.

'If you want something extra,' Retana said, 'go and get it. There will be a regular cuadrilla out there. Bring as many of your own pics as you want. The charlotada is over by 10.30.'

'All right,' Manuel said. 'If that's the way you feel about it.'

'That's the way,' Retana said.

'I'll see you tomorrow night,' Manuel said.

'I'll be out there,' Retana said.

Manuel picked up his suitcase and went out.

'Shut the door,' Retana called.

Manuel looked back. Retana was sitting forward looking at some papers. Manuel pulled the door tight until it clicked.

He went down the stairs and out of the door into the hot brightness of the street. It was very hot in the street and the light on the white buildings was sudden and hard on his eyes. He walked down the shady side of the steep street towards the Puerta del Sol. The shade felt solid and cool as running water. The heat came suddenly as he crossed the intersecting streets. Manuel saw no one he knew in all the people he passed.

Just before the Puerto del Sol he turned into a café.

It was quiet in the café. There were a few men sitting at tables against the wall. At one table four men played cards. Most of the men sat against the wall smoking, empty coffee-cups and liqueur-glasses before them on the tables. Manuel went through the long room to a small room in back. A man sat at a table in the corner asleep. Manuel sat down at one of the tables.

A waiter came in and stood beside Manuel's table.

'Have you seen Zurito?' Manuel asked him.

'He was in before lunch,' the waiter answered. 'He won't be back before five o'clock.'

'Bring me some coffee and milk and a shot of the ordinary,' Manuel said.

The waiter came back into the room carrying a tray with a big coffee-glass and a liqueur-glass on it. In his left hand he held a bottle of brandy. He swung these down to the table and a boy who had followed him poured coffee and milk into the glass from two shiny, spouted pots with long handles.

Manuel took off his cap and the waiter noticed his pigtail pinned forward on his head. He winked at the coffee-boy as he poured out the brandy into the little glass beside Manuel's coffee. The coffee-boy looked at Manuel's pale face curiously.

'You fighting here?' asked the waiter, corking up the bottle.

'Yes,' Manuel said. 'Tomorrow.'

The waiter stood there, holding the bottle on one hip.

'You in the Charlie Chaplin's?' he asked.

The coffee-boy looked away, embarrassed.

'No. In the ordinary.'

'I thought they were going to have Chaves and Hernandez,' the waiter said.

'No. Me and another.'

'Who? Chaves or Hernandez?'

'Hernandez, I think.'

13

'What's the matter with Chaves?'

'He got hurt.'

'Where did you hear that?'

'Retana.'

'Hey, Looie,' the waiter called to the next room, 'Chaves got cogida.'

Manuel had taken the wrapper off the lumps of sugar and dropped them into his coffee. He stirred it and drank it down, sweet, hot, and warming in his empty stomach. He drank off the brandy.

'Give me another shot of that,' he said to the waiter.

The waiter uncorked the bottle and poured the glass full, slopping another drink into the saucer. Another waiter had come up in front of the table. The coffee-boy was gone.

'Is Chaves hurt bad?' the second waiter asked Manuel.

'I don't know,' Manuel said, 'Retana didn't say.'

'A hell of a lot he cares,' the tall waiter said. Manuel had not seen him before. He must have just come up.

'If you stand in with Retana in this town, you're a made man,' the tall waiter said. 'If you aren't in with him, you might just as well go out and shoot yourself.'

'You said it,' the other waiter who had come in said. 'You said it then.'

'You're right I said it,' said the tall waiter. 'I know what I'm talking about when I talk about that bird.'

'Look what he's done for Villalta,' the first waiter said.

'And that ain't all,' the tall waiter said. 'Look what he's done for Marcial Lalanda. Look what he's done for Nacional.'

'You said it, kid,' agreed the short waiter.

Manuel looked at them, standing talking in front of his table. He had drunk his second brandy. They had forgotten about him. They were not interested in him.

'Look at that bunch of camels,' the tall waiter went on. 'Did you ever see this Nacional II?'

'I seen him last Sunday, didn't I?' the original waiter said.

'He's a giraffe,' the short waiter said.

'What did I tell you?' the tall waiter said. 'Those are Retana's boys.'

'Say, give me another shot of that,' Manuel said. He had

poured the brandy the waiter had slopped over in the saucer into his glass and drank it while they were talking.

The original waiter poured his glass full mechanically, and the three of them went out of the room talking.

In the far corner the man was still asleep, snoring slightly on the intaking breath, his head back against the wall.

Manuel drank his brandy. He felt sleepy himself. It was too hot to go out into the town. Besides there was nothing to do. He wanted to see Zurito. He would go to sleep while he waited. He kicked his suitcase under the table to be sure it was there. Perhaps it would be better to put it back under the seat, against the wall. He leaned down and shoved it under. Then he leaned forward on the table and went to sleep.

When he woke there was someone sitting across the table from him. It was a big man with a heavy brown face like an Indian. He had been sitting there some time. He had waved the waiter away and sat reading the paper and occasionally looking down at Manuel, asleep, his head on the table. He read the paper laboriously forming the words with his lips as he read. When it tired him he looked at Manuel. He sat heavily in the chair, his black Cordoba hat tipped forward.

Manuel sat up and looked at him.

'Hello, Zurito,' he said.

'Hello, kid,' the big man said.

'I've been asleep.' Manuel rubbed his forehead with the back of his fist.

'I thought maybe you were.'

'How's everything?'

'Good. How is everything with you?'

'Not so good.'

They were both silent. Zurito, the picador, looked at Manuel's white face. Manuel looked down at the picador's enormous hands folding the paper to put away in his pocket.

'I got a favour to ask you, Manos,' Manuel said.

Manosduros was Zurito's nickname. He never heard it without thinking of his huge hands. He put them forward on the table self-consciously.

'Let's have a drink,' he said.

'Sure,' said Manuel.

The waiter came and went and came again. He went out of the room looking back at the two men at the table.

'What's the matter, Manolo?' Zurito set down his glass.

'Would you pic two bulls for me tomorrow night?' Manuel asked, looking at Zurito across the table.

'No,' said Zurito. 'I'm not pic-ing.'

Manuel looked down at his glass. He had expected that answer; now he had it. Well, he had it.

'I'm sorry, Manolo, but I'm not pic-ing.' Zurito looked at his hands.

'That's all right,' Manuel said.

'I'm too old,' Zurito said.

'I just asked you,' Manuel said.

'Is it the nocturnal tomorrow?'

'That's it. I figured if I had just one good.pic, I could get away with it.'

'How much are you getting?'

'Three hundred pesetas.'

'I get more than that for pic-ing.'

'I know,' said Manuel. 'I didn't have any right to ask you.'

'What do you keep on doing it for?' Zurito asked. 'Why don't you cut off your coleta, Manolo?'

'I don't know,' Manuel said.

'You're pretty near as old as I am,' Zurito said.

'I don't know,' Manuel said. 'I got to do it. If I can fix it so that I get an even break, that's all I want. I got to stick with it, Manos.'

'No you don't.'

'Yes, I do. I've tried keeping away from it.'

'I know how you feel. But it isn't right. You ought to get out and stay out.'

'I can't do it. Besides, I've been going good lately.'

Zurito looked at his face.

'You've been in the hospital.'

'But I was going great when I got hurt.'

Zurito said nothing. He tipped the cognac out of his saucer into his glass.

'The papers said they never saw a better faena,' Manuel said.

Zurito looked at him.

'You know when I get going I'm good,' Manuel said.

'You're too old,' the picador said.

'No,' said Manuel. 'You're ten years older than I am.'

'With me it's different.'

'I'm not too old,' Manuel said.

They sat silent, Manuel watching the picador's face.

'I was going great till I got hurt,' Manuel offered.

'You ought to have seen me, Manos,' Manuel said, reproachfully.

'I don't want to see you.' Zurito said. 'It makes me nervous.'

'You haven't seen me lately.'

'I've seen you plenty.'

Zurito looked at Manuel, avoiding his eyes.

'You ought to quit it, Manolo.'

'I can't,' Manuel said. 'I'm going good now, I tell you.'

Zurito leaned forward, his hands on the table.

'Listen. I'll pic for you and if you don't go big tomorrow night, you'll quit. See? Will you do that?'

'Sure.'

Zurito leaned back, relieved.

'You got to quit,' he said. 'No monkey business. You got to cut the coleta.'

'I won't have to quit,' Manuel said. 'You watch me. I've got the stuff.'

Zurito stood up. He felt tired from arguing.

'You got to quit,' he said. 'I'll cut your coleta myself.'

'No, you won't,' Manuel said. 'You won't have a chance.'

Zurito called the waiter.

'Come on,' said Zurito. 'Come on up to the house.'

Manuel reached under the seat for his suitcase. He was happy. He knew Zurito would pic for him. He was the best picador living. It was all simple now.

'Come on up to the house and we'll eat,' Zurito said.

Manuel stood in the patio de caballos waiting for the Charlie Chaplin to be over. Zurito stood beside him. Where they stood it was dark. The high door that led into the bull-ring was shut. Above them they heard a shout, then another shout of laughter. Then there was silence. Manuel liked the smell of the stables about the patio de caballos. It smelt good in the dark. There was another roar from the arena and then applause, prolonged applause, going on and on.

'You ever seen these fellows?' Zurito asked, big and looming beside Manuel in the dark.

'No,' Manuel said.

'They're pretty funny,' Zurito said. He smiled to himself in the dark.

The high, double, tight-fitting door into the bull-ring swung open and Manuel saw the ring in the hard light of the arc-lights, the plaza, dark all the way around, rising high; around the edge of the ring were running and bowing two men dressed like tramps, followed by a third in the uniform of a hotel bell-boy who stooped and picked up the hats and canes thrown down onto the sand and tossed them back up into the darkness.

The electric light went on in the patio.

'I'll climb onto one of those ponies while you collect the kids,' Zurito said.

Behind them came the jingle of the mules, coming out to go into the arena and be hitched onto the dead bull.

The members of the cuadrilla, who had been watching the burlesque from the runway between the barrera and the seats, came walking back and stood in a group talking, under the electric light in the patio. A good-looking lad in a silver-and-orange suit came up to Manuel and smiled.

'I'm Hernandez,' he said and put out his hand.

Manuel shook it.

'They're regular elephants we've got tonight,' the boy said cheerfully.

'They're big ones with horns,' Manuel agreed.

'You drew the worst lot,' the boy said.

'That's all right,' Manuel said. 'The bigger they are, the more meat for the poor.'

'Where did you get that one?' Hernandez grinned.

'That's an old one,' Manuel said. 'You line up your cuadrilla, so I can see what I've got.'

'You've got some good kids,' Hernandez said. He was very cheerful. He had been on twice before in nocturnals and was beginning to get a following in Madrid. He was happy the fight would start in a few minutes.

'Where are the pics?' Manuel asked.

'They're back in the corrals fighting about who gets the beautiful horses,' Hernandez grinned.

The mules came through the gate in a rush, the whips snapping, bells jangling and the young bull ploughing a furrow of sand.

They formed up for the paseo as soon as the bull had gone through.

Manuel and Hernandez stood in front. The youths of the cuadrillas were behind, their heavy capes furled over their arms. In back, the four picadors, mounted, holding their steel-tipped push-poles erect in the half-dark of the corral.

'It's a wonder Retana wouldn't give us enough light to see the horses by,' one picador said.

'He knows we'll be happier if we don't get too good a look at these skins,' another pic answered.

'This thing I'm on barely keeps me off the ground,' the first picador said.

'Well, they're horses.'

'Sure, they're horses.'

They talked, sitting their gaunt horses in the dark.

Zurito said nothing. He had the only steady horse of the lot. He had tried him, wheeling him in the corrals and he responded to the bit and the spurs. He had taken the bandage off his right eye and cut the strings where they had tied his ears tight shut and the base. He was a good, solid horse, solid on his legs. That was all he needed. He intended to ride him all through the corrida. He had already, since he had mounted, sitting in the half-dark in the big, quilted saddle, waiting for the paseo, pic-ed through the whole corrida in his mind. The other picadors went on talking on both sides of him. He did not hear them.

The two matadors stood together in front of their three peones, their capes furled over their left arms in the same fashion. Manuel was thinking about the three lads in back of him. They were all three Madrilenos, like Hernandez, boys about nineteen. One of them, a gypsy, serious, aloof, and dark-faced, he liked the look of. He turned.

'What's your name, kid?' he asked the gypsy.

'Fuentes,' the gypsy said.

'That's a good name,' Manuel said.

The gypsy smiled, showing his teeth.

'You take the bull and give him a little run when he comes out,' Manuel said.

'All right,' the gypsy said. His face was serious. He began to think about just what he would do.

'Here she goes,' Manuel said to Hernandez.

'All right. We'll go.'

Heads up, swinging with the music, their right arms swinging free, they stepped out, crossing the sanded arena under the arc-lights, the cuadrillas opening out behind, the picadors riding after, behind came the bull-ring servants and the jingling mules. The crowd applauded Hernandez as they marched across the arena. Arrogant, swinging, they looked straight ahead as they marched.

They bowed before the president, and the procession broke-up into its component parts. The bullfighters went over to the barrera and changed their heavy mantles for the light fighting capes. The mules went out. The picadors galloped jerkily around the ring, and two rode out the gate they had come in by. The servants swept the sand smooth.

Manuel drank a glass of water poured for him by one of Retana's deputies, who was acting as his manager and sword-handler. Hernandez came over from speaking with his own manager.

'You got a good hand, kid,' Manuel complimented him.

'They like me,' Hernandez said happily.

'How did the paseo go?' Manuel asked Retana's man.

'Like a wedding,' said the handler. 'Fine. You came out like Joselito and Belmonte.'

Zurito rode by, a bulky equestrian statue. He wheeled his horse and faced him towards the toril on the far side of the ring where the bull would come out. It was strange under the arc-light. He pic-ed in the hot afternoon sun for big money. He didn't like this arc-light business. He wished they would get started.

Manuel went up to him.

'Pic him, Manos,' he said. 'Cut him down to size for me.'

'I'll pic him, kid,' Zurito spat on the sand. 'I'll make him jump out of the ring.'

'Lean on him, Manos,' Manuel said.

'I'll lean on him,' Zurito said. 'What's holding it up?'

'He's coming now,' Manuel said.

Zurito sat there, his feet in the box-stirrups, his great legs in the buckskin-covered armour gripping the horse, the reins in his left hand, the long pic held in his right hand, his broad hat well down over his eyes to shade them from the lights, watching the distant door of the toril. His horse's ears quivered. Zurito patted him with his left hand.

The red door of the toril swung back and for a moment Zurito looked into the empty passage-way far across the arena. Then the bull came out in a rush, skidding on his four legs as he came out under the lights, then charging in a gallop, moving softly in a fast gallop, silent except as he woofed through wide nostrils as he charged, glad to be free after the dark pen.

In the first row of seats, slightly bored, leaning forward to write on the cement wall in front of his knees, the substitute bullfight critic of *El Heraldo* scribbled: 'Campagnero, Negro, 42, came out at 90 miles an hour with plenty of gas –'

Manuel, leaning against the barrera, watching the bull, waved his hand and the gypsy ran out, trailing his cape. The bull, in full gallop, pivoted and charged the cape, his head down, his tail rising. The gypsy moved in a zig-zag, and as he passed, the bull caught sight of him and abandoned the cape to charge the man. The gyp sprinted and vaulted the red fence of the barrera as the bull struck it with his horns. He tossed into it twice with his horns, banging into the wood blindly.

The critic of *El Heraldo* lit a cigarette and tossed the match at the bull, then wrote in his note-book, 'large and with enough horns to satisfy the cash customers, Campagnero showed a tendency to cut into the terrain of the bullfighters.'

Manuel stepped out on the hard sand as the bull banged into the fence. Out of the corner of his eye he saw Zurito sitting the white horse close to the barrera, about a quarter of the way around the ring to the left. Manuel held the cape close in front of him, a fold in each hand, and shouted at the bull. 'Huh! Huh!' The bull turned, seemed to brace against the fence as he charged in a scramble, driving into the cape as Manuel side-stepped, pivoted on his heels with the charge of the bull, and swung the cape just ahead of the horns. At the end of the cape he was facing the bull again and held the cape in the same position close in front of his body, and pivoted again as the bull recharged. Each time, as he swung, the crowd shouted.

Four times he swung with the bull, lifting the cape so it billowed full, and each time bringing the bull around to charge again. Then, at the end of the fifth swing, he held the cape against his hip and pivoted, so the cape swung out like a ballet dancer's skirt and wound the bull around himself like a belt, to step clear, leaving the bull facing Zurito on the white horse, come up and planted firm, the horse facing the bull, its ears forward, its lips nervous. Zurito, his hat over his eyes, leaning forward, the long pole sticking out before and behind in a sharp angle under his right arm, held half-way down, the triangular iron point facing the bull.

El Heraldo's second-string critic, drawing on his cigarette, his eyes on the bull, wrote: 'the veteran Manolo designed a series of acceptable veronicas, ending in a very Belmontistic recorte that earned applause from the regulars, and we entered the tercio of the cavalry.'

Zurito sat his horse, measuring the distance between the bull and the end of the pic. As he looked, the bull gathered himself together and charged, his eyes on the horse's chest. As he lowered his head to hook, Zurito sunk the point of the pic in the swelling hump of muscle above the bull's shoulder, leaned all his weight on the shaft, and with his left hand pulled the white horse into the air, front hoofs pawing, and swung him to the right as he pushed the bull under and through so the horns passed safely under the horse's belly and the horse came down, quivering, the bull's tail brushing his chest as he charged the cape Hernandez offered him.

Hernandez ran sideways, taking the bull out and away with the cape, towards the other picador. He fixed him with a swing of the cape, squarely facing the horse and rider, and stepped back. As the bull saw the horse he charged. The picador's lance slid along his back, and as the shock of the charge lifted the horse, the picador was already halfway out of the saddle, lifting his right leg clear as he missed with the lance and falling to the left side to keep the horse between him and the bull. The horse, lifted and gored, crashed over with the bull driving into him, the picador gave a shove with his boots against the horse and lay clear, waiting to be lifted and hauled away and put on his feet.

Manuel let the bull drive into the fallen horse; he was in no hurry, the picador was safe; besides, it did a picador like that good to worry. He'd stay on longer next time. Lousy pics! He looked across the sand at Zurito a little way out from the barrera, his horse rigid, waiting.

'Huh!' he called to the bull. 'Tomar!' holding the cape in both hands so it would catch his eye. The bull detached himself from the horse and charged the cape, and Manuel, running sideways and holding the cape spread wide, stopped, swung on his heels, and brought the bull sharply around facing Zurito.

'Campagnero accepted a pair of varas for the death of one rosinante, with Hernandez and Manolo at the quites,' *El Heraldo*'s critic wrote. 'He pressed on the iron and clearly showed he was no horse-lover. The veteran Zurito resurrected some of his old stuff with the pike-pole, notably the suerte –'

'Olé! Olé!' the man sitting beside him shouted. The shout was lost in the roar of the crowd, and he slapped the critic on the back. The critic looked up to see Zurito, directly below him, leaning far out over his horse, the length of the pic rising in a sharp angle under his armpit, holding the pic almost by the point, bearing down with all his weight, holding the bull off, the bull pushing and driving to get at the horse, and Zurito, far out, on top of him, holding him, holding him, and slowly pivoting the horse against the pressure, so that at last he was clear. Zurito felt the moment when the horse was clear and the bull could come past, and relaxed the absolute steel lock of his resistance, and the triangular steel point of the pic ripped in the bull's hump of shoulder muscle as he tore loose to find Hernandez's cape before his muzzle. He charged blindly into the cape and the boy took him out into the open arena.

Zurito sat patting his horse and looking at the bull charging the cape that Hernandez swung for him out under the bright light while the crowd shouted.

'You see that one?' he said to Manuel.

'It was a wonder,' Manuel said.

'I got him that time,' Zurito said. 'Look at him now.'

At the conclusion of a closely turned pass of the cape the bull slid to his knees. He was up at once, but far out across the sand Manuel and Zurito saw the shine of the pumping flow of blood, smooth against the black of the bull's shoulder.

'I got him that time,' Zurito said.

'He's a good bull,' Manuel said.

'If they gave me another shot at him, I'd kill him,' Zurito said.

'They'll change the thirds on us,' Manuel said.

'Look at him now,' Zurito said.

'I got to go over there,' Manuel said, and started on a run for the other side of the ring, where the monos were leading a horse out by the bridle towards the bull, whacking him on the legs with rods and all, in a procession, trying to get him towards the bull, who stood, dropping his head, pawing, unable to make up his mind to charge.

Zurito, sitting his horse, walking him towards the scene, not missing any detail, scowled.

Finally the bull charged, the horse leaders ran for the barrera, the picador hit too far back, and the bull got under the horse, lifted him, threw him onto his back.

Zurito watched. The monos, in their red shirts, running out to drag the picador clear. The picador, now on his feet, swearing and flopping his arms. Manuel and Hernandez standing ready with their capes. And the bull, the great, black bull, with a horse on his back, hooves dangling, the bridle caught in the horns. Black bull with a horse on his back staggering short-legged, then arching his neck and lifting, thrusting, charging to slide the horse off, horse sliding down. Then the bull into a lunging charge at the cape Manuel spread for him.

The bull was slower now, Manuel felt. He was bleeding badly. There was a sheen of blood all down his flank.

Manuel offered him the cape again. There he came, eyes open, ugly, watching the cape. Manuel stepped to the side and raised his arms, tightening the cape ahead of the bull for the veronica.

Now he was facing the bull. Yes, his head was going down a little. He was carrying it lower. That was Zurito.

Manuel flopped the cape; there he comes; he side-stepped and swung in another veronica. He's shooting awfully accurately, he thought. He's had enough fight, so he's watching now. He's hunting now. Got his eye on me. But I always give him the cape.

He shook the cape at the bull; there he comes; he side-stepped. Awful close that time. I don't want to work that close to him.

The edge of the cape was set with blood where it had swept along the bull's back as he went by.

All right, here's the last one.

Manuel, facing the bull, having turned with him each charge, offered the cape with his two hands. The bull looked at him. Eyes watching, horns straight forward, the bull looked at him, watching.

'Huh!' Manuel said, 'Toro!' and leaning back, swung the cape forward. Here he comes. He side-stepped, swung the cape in back of him, and pivoted, so the bull followed a swirl of cape and then was left with nothing, fixed by the pass, dominated by the cape. Manuel swung the cape under his muzzle with one hand, to show the bull was fixed, and walked away.

There was no applause.

Manuel walked across the sand towards the barrera, while Zurito rode out of the ring. The trumpet had blown to change the act to the planting of the banderillos while Manuel had been working with the bull. He had not consciously noticed it. The monos were spreading canvas over the two dead horses and sprinkling sawdust around them.

Manuel came up to the barrera for a drink of water. Retana's man handed him the heavy porous jug.

Fuentes, the tall gypsy, was standing holding a pair of banderillos, holding them together, slim, red sticks, fish-hook points out. He looked at Manuel.

'Go on out there,' Manuel said.

The gypsy trotted out. Manuel set down the jug and watched. He wiped his face with his handkerchief.

The critic of *El Heraldo* reached for the bottle of warm champagne that stood between his feet, took a drink, and finished his paragraph.

'– the aged Manolo rated no applause for a vulgar series of lances with the cape and we entered the third of the palings.'

Alone in the centre of the ring the bull stood, still fixed. Fuentes, tall, flat-backed, walking towards him arrogantly, his arms spread out, the two slim, red sticks, one in each hand, held by the fingers, points straight forward. Fuentes walked forward. Back of him and to one side was a peon with a cape. The bull looked at him and was no longer fixed.

His eyes watched Fuentes, now standing still. Now he leaned back, calling to him. Fuentes twitched the two banderillos and the light on the steel points caught the bull's eye.

His tail went up and he charged.

He came straight, his eyes on the man. Fuentes stood still, leaning back, the banderillos pointing forward. As the bull lowered his head to hook, Fuentes leaned backward, his arms came together and rose, his two hands touching, the banderillos two descending red lines, and leaning forward drove the points into the bull's shoulder, leaning far in over the bull's horns and pivoting on the two upright sticks, his legs tight together, his body curving to one side to let the bull pass.

'Olé!' from the crowd.

The bull was hooking wildly, jumping like a trout, all four feet off the ground. The red shafts of the banderillos tossed as he jumped.

Manuel standing at the barrera, noticed that he hooked always to the right.

'Tell him to drop the next pair on the right,' he said to the kid who started to run out to Fuentes with the new banderillos.

A heavy hand fell on his shoulder. It was Zurito.

'How do you feel, kid?' he asked.

Manuel was watching the bull.

Zurito leaned forward on the barrera, leaning the weight of his body on his arms. Manuel turned to him.

'You're going good,' Zurito said.

Manuel shook his head. He had nothing to do now until the next third. The gypsy was very good with the banderillos. The bull would come to him in the next third in good shape. He was a good bull. It had all been easy up to now. The final stuff with the sword was all he worried over. He did not really worry. He did not even think about it. But standing there he had a heavy sense of apprehension. He looked out at the bull, planning his faena, his work with the red cloth that was to reduce the bull, to make him manageable.

The gypsy was walking out towards the bull again, walking heel-and-toe, insultingly, like a ballroom dancer, the red shafts of the banderillos twitching with his walk. The bull watched him, not fixed now, hunting him, but waiting to get close enough so he could be sure of getting him, getting the horns into him.

As Fuentes walked forward the bull charged. Fuentes ran across the quarter of a circle as the bull charged and, as he passed running backwards, stopped, swung forward, rose on his toes, arms straight out, and sunk the banderillos straight down into the tight of the big shoulder muscles as the bull missed him.

The crowd were wild about it.

'That kid won't stay in this night stuff long,' Retana's man said to Zurito.

'He's good,' Zurito said.

'Watch him now.'

They watched.

Fuentes was standing with his back against the barrera. Two of the cuadrilla were back of him, with their capes ready to flop over the fence to distract the bull.

The bull, with his tongue out, his barrel heaving, was watching the gypsy. He thought he had him now. Back against the red planks. Only a short charge away. The bull watched him.

The gypsy bent back, drew back his arms, the banderillos

pointing at the bull. He called to the bull, stamped one foot. The bull was suspicious. He wanted the man. No more barbs in the shoulder.

Fuentes walked a little closer to the bull. Bent back. Called again. Somebody in the crowd shouted a warning.

'He's too damn close,' Zurito said.

'Watch him,' Retana's man said.

Leaning back, inciting the bull with the banderillos, Fuentes jumped, both feet off the ground. As he jumped the bull's tail rose and he charged. Fuentes came down on his toes, arms straight out, whole body arching forward, and drove the shafts straight down as he swung his body clear of the right horn.

The bull crashed into the barrera where the flopping capes had attracted his eye as he lost the man.

The gypsy came running along the barrera towards Manuel, taking the applause of the crowd. His vest was ripped where he had not quite cleared the point of the horn. He was happy about it, showing it to the spectators. He made a tour of the ring. Zurito saw him go by, smiling, pointing to his vest. He smiled.

Somebody else was planting the last pair of banderillos. Nobody was paying any attention.

Retana's man tucked a baton inside the red cloth of a muleta, folded the cloth over it, and handed it over the barrera to Manuel. He reached in the leather sword-case, took out a sword, and holding it by its leather scabbard, reached it over the fence to Manuel. Manuel pulled the blade out by the red hilt and the scabbard fell limp.

He looked at Zurito. The big man saw he was sweating.

'Now you get him, kid,' Zurito said.

Manuel nodded.

'He's in good shape,' Zurito said.

'Just like you want him,' Retana's man assured him.

Manuel nodded.

The trumpeter, up under the roof, blew for the final act, and Manuel walked across the arena towards where, up in the dark boxes, the president must be.

In the front row seats the substitute bullfight critic of *El*

Heraldo took a long drink of the warm champagne. He had decided it was not worth while to write a running story and would write up the corrida back in the office. What the hell was it anyway? Only a nocturnal. If he missed anything he would get it out of the morning papers. He took another drink of the champagne. He had a date at Maxim's at twelve. Who were these bullfighters anyway? Kids and bums. A bunch of bums. He put his pad of paper in his pocket and looked over towards Manuel, standing very much alone in the ring, gesturing with his hat in a salute towards a box he could not see high up in the dark plaza. Out in the ring the bull stood quiet, looking at nothing.

'I dedicate this bull to you, Mr President, and to the public of Madrid, the most intelligent and generous in the world,' was what Manuel was saying. It was a formula. He said it all. It was a little long for nocturnal use.

He bowed at the dark, straightened, tossed his hat over his shoulder, and, carrying the muleta in his left hand and the sword in his right, walked out towards the bull.

Manuel walked towards the bull. The bull looked at him; his eyes were quick. Manuel noticed the way the banderillos hung down on his left shoulder and the steady sheen of blood from Zurito's pic-ing. He noticed the way the bull's feet were. As he walked forward, holding the muleta in his left hand and the sword in his right, he watched the bull's feet. The bull could not charge without gathering his feet together. Now he stood square on them, dully.

Manuel walked towards him, watching his feet. This was all right. He could do this. He must work to get the bull's head down, so he could go in past the horns and kill him. He did not think about the sword, not about killing the bull. He thought about one thing at a time. The coming things oppressed him, though. Walking forward, watching the bull's feet, he saw successively his eyes, his wet muzzle, and the wide, forward-pointing spread of his horns. The bull had light circles about his eyes. His eyes watched Manuel. He felt he was going to get this little one with the white face.

Standing still now and spreading the red cloth of the muleta with the sword, pricking the point into the cloth so that the sword, now held in his left hand, spread the red flannel like the jib of a boat, Manuel noticed the points of the bull's horns. One of them was splintered from banging against the barrera. The other was sharp as a porcupine quill. Manuel noticed while spreading the muleta that the white base of the horn was stained red. While he noticed these things he did not lose sight of the bull's feet. The bull watched Manuel steadily.

He's on the defensive now, Manuel thought. He's reserving himself. I've got to bring him out of that and get his head down. Always get his head down. Zurito had his head down once, but he's come back. He'll bleed when I start him going and that will bring it down.

Holding the muleta, with the sword in his left hand widening it in front of him, he called to the bull.

The bull looked at him.

He leaned back insultingly and shook the widespread flannel.

The bull saw the muleta. It was a bright scarlet under the arc-light. The bull's legs tightened.

Here he comes. Whoosh! Manuel turned as the bull came and raised the muleta so that it passed over the bull's horns and swept down his broad back from head to tail. The bull had gone clean up in the air with the charge. Manuel had not moved.

At the end of the pass the bull turned like a cat coming around a corner and faced Manuel.

He was on the offensive again. His heaviness was gone. Manuel noted the fresh blood shining down the black shoulder and dripping down the bull's leg. He drew the sword out of the muleta and held it in his right hand. The muleta held low down in his left hand, leaning towards the left, he called to the bull. The bull's legs tightened, his eyes on the muleta. Here he comes, Manuel thought. Yuh!

He swung with the charge, sweeping the muleta ahead of the bull, his feet firm, the sword following the curve, a point of light under the arcs.

The bull recharged as the pase natural finished and Manuel raised the muleta for a pase de pecho. Firmly planted, the bull came by his chest under the raised muleta. Manuel leaned his head back to avoid the clattering banderillo shafts. The hot, black bull body touched his chest as it passed.

Too damn close, Manuel thought. Zurito, leaning on the barrera, spoke rapidly to the gypsy who trotted out towards Manuel with a cape. Zurito pulled his hat down low and looked out across the arena at Manuel.

Manuel was facing the bull again, the muleta held low and to the left. The bull's head was down as he watched the muleta.

'If it was Belmonte doing that stuff, they'd go crazy,' Retana's man said.

Zurito said nothing. He was watching Manuel out in the centre of the arena.

'Where did the boss dig this fellow up?' Retana's man asked.

'Out of the hospital,' Zurito said.

'That's where he's going damn quick,' Retana's man said.

Zurito turned on him.

'Knock on that,' he said, pointing to the barrera.

'I was just kidding, man,' Retana's man said.

'Knock on the wood.'

Retana's man leaned forward and knocked three times on the barrera.

'Watch the faena,' Zurito said.

Out in the centre of the ring, under the lights, Manuel was kneeling, facing the bull, and as he raised the muleta in both hands the bull charged, tail up.

Manuel swung his body clear and, as the bull recharged, brought around the muleta in a half-circle that pulled the bull to his knees.

'Why, that one's a great bullfighter,' Retana's man said.

'No, he's not,' said Zurito.

Manuel stood up and, the muleta in his left hand, the sword in his right, acknowledged the applause from the dark plaza.

The bull had humped himself up from his knees and stood waiting, his head hung low.

Zurito spoke to two of the other lads of the cuadrilla and they ran out to stand back of Manuel with their capes. There were four men back of him now. Hernandez had followed him since he first came out with the muleta. Fuentes stood watching, his cape held against his body, tall, in repose, watching lazy-eyed. Now the two came up. Hernandez motioned them to stand one at each side. Manuel stood alone, facing the bull.

Manuel waved back the men with the capes. Stepping back cautiously, they saw his face was white and sweating.

Didn't they know enough to keep back? Did they want to catch the bull's eye with the capes after he was fixed and ready? He had enough to worry about without that kind of thing.

The bull was standing, his four feet square, looking at the muleta. Manuel furled the muleta in his left hand. The bull's eyes watched it. His body was heavy on his feet. He carried his head low, but not too low.

Manuel lifted the muleta at him. The bull did not move. Only his eyes watched.

He's all lead, Manuel thought. He's all square. He's framed right. He'll take it.

He thought in bullfight terms. Sometimes he had a thought and the particular piece of slang would not come into his mind and he could not realize the thought. His instincts and his knowledge worked automatically, and his brain worked slowly and in words. He knew all about bulls. He did not have to think about them. He just did the right thing. His eyes noted things and his body performed the necessary measures without thought. If he thought about it, he would be gone.

Now, facing the bull, he was conscious of many things at the same time. There were the horns, the one splintered, the other smoothly sharp, the need to profile himself towards the left horn, lance himself short and straight, lower the muleta so the bull would follow it, and, going in over the horns, put the sword all the way into a little spot about as big as a five-peseta piece straight in back of the neck, between the sharp pitch of the bull's shoulders. He must do all this and must then come out from between the horns. He was conscious he must do all this, but his only thought was in words: 'Corto y derecho.'

'Corto y derecho,' he thought, furling the muleta. Short and straight. Corto y derecho, he drew the sword out of the muleta, profiled on the splintered left horn, dropped the muleta across his body, so his right hand with the sword on the level with his eye made the sign of the cross, and, rising on his toes, sighted along the dipping blade of the sword at the spot high up between the bull's shoulders.

Corto y derecho he lanced himself on the bull.

There was a shock, and he felt himself go up in the air. He pushed on the sword as he went up and over, and it flew out of his hand. He hit the ground and the bull was on him. Manuel, lying on the ground, kicked at the bull's muzzle with his slippered feet. Kicking, kicking, the bull after him, missing him in his excitement, bumping him with his head, driving the horns into the sand. Kicking like a man keeping a ball in the air, Manuel kept the bull from getting a clean thrust at him.

Manuel felt the wind on his back from the capes flopping at the bull, and then the bull was gone, gone over him in a rush. Dark, as his belly went over. Not even stepped on.

Manuel stood up and picked up the muleta. Fuentes handed him the sword. It was bent where it had struck the shoulder-blade. Manuel straightened it on his knee and ran towards the bull, standing now beside one of the dead horses. As he ran, his jacket flopped where it had been ripped under his armpit.

'Get him out of there,' Manuel shouted to the gypsy. The bull had smelled the blood of the dead horse and ripped into the canvas cover with his horns. He charged Fuentes's cape, with the canvas hanging from his splintered horn, and the crowd laughed. Out in the ring, he tossed his head to rid himself of the canvas. Hernandez, running up from behind him, grabbed the end of the canvas and neatly lifted it off the horn.

The bull followed it in a half-charge and stopped still. He was on the defensive again. Manuel was walking towards him with the sword and muleta. Manuel swung the muleta before him. The bull would not charge.

Manuel profiled towards the bull, sighting along the dipping blade of the sword. The bull was motionless, seemingly dead on his feet, incapable of another charge.

Manuel rose to his toes, sighting along the steel, and charged.

Again there was the shock and he felt himself being borne back in a rush, to strike hard on the sand. There was no chance of kicking this time. The bull was on top of him. Manuel lay as though dead, his head on his arms, and the bull bumped him. Bumped his back, bumped his face in the sand. He felt the horn go into the sand between his folded arms. The bull hit him in the small of the back. His face drove into the sand. The horn drove through one of his sleeves and the bull ripped it off. Manuel was tossed clear and the bull followed the capes.

Manuel got up, found the sword and muleta, tried the point of the sword with his thumb, and then ran towards the barrera for a new sword.

Retana's man handed him the sword over the edge of the barrera.

'Wipe off your face,' he said.

Manuel, running again towards the bull, wiped his bloody face with his handkerchief. He had not seen Zurito. Where was Zurito?

The cuadrilla had stepped away from the bull and waited with their capes. The bull stood, heavy and dull again after the action.

Manuel walked towards him with the muleta. He stopped and shook it. The bull did not respond. He passed it right and left, left and right before the bull's muzzle. The bull's eyes watched it and turned with the swing, but he would not charge. He was waiting for Manuel.

Manuel was worried. There was nothing to do but go in. Corto y derecho. He profiled close to the bull, crossed the muleta in front of his body and charged. As he pushed in the sword, he jerked his body to the left to clear the horn. The bull passed him and the sword shot up in the air, twinkling under the arc-lights, to fall red-hilted on the sand.

Manuel ran over and picked it up. It was bent and he straightened it over his knee.

As he came running towards the bull, fixed again now, he passed Hernandez standing with his cape.

'He's all bone,' the boy said encouragingly.

Manuel nodded, wiping his face. He put the bloody handkerchief in his pocket.

There was the bull. He was close to the barrera now. Damn him. Maybe he was all bone. Maybe there was not any place for the sword to go in. The hell there wasn't! He'd show them.

He tried a pass with the muleta and the bull did not move. Manuel chopped the muleta back and forth in front of the bull. Nothing doing.

He furled the muleta, drew the sword out, profiled and drove in on the bull. He felt the sword buckle as he shoved it in, leaning his weight on it, and then it shot in the air, end-over-ending into the crowd. Manuel had jerked clear as the sword jumped.

The first cushions thrown down out of the dark missed him. Then one hit him in the face, his bloody face looking towards the crowd. They were coming down fast. Spotting the sand. Somebody threw an empty champagne-bottle from close range. It hit Manuel on the foot. He stood there watching the dark, where the things were coming from. Then something whished through the air and struck by him. Manuel leaned over and picked it up. It was his sword. He straightened it over his knee and gestured with it to the crowd.

'Thank you,' he said. 'Thank you.'

Oh, the dirty bastards! Dirty bastards! Oh, the lousy, dirty bastards! He kicked into a cushion as he ran.

There was the bull. The same as ever. All right, you dirty, lousy bastard!

Manuel passed the muleta in front of the bull's black muzzle.

Nothing doing.

You won't. All right. He stepped close and jammed the sharp peak of the muleta into the bull's damp muzzle.

The bull was on him as he jumped back and as he tripped on a cushion he felt the horn go into him, into his side. He grabbed the horn with his two hands and rode backward, holding tight onto the place. The bull tossed him and he was clear. He lay still. It was all right. The bull was gone.

He got up coughing and feeling broken and gone. The dirty bastards!

'Give me the sword,' he shouted.' Give me the stuff.'

Fuentes came up with the muleta and the sword.

Hernandez put his arm around him.

'Go on to the infirmary, man,' he said. 'Don't be a damn fool.'

35

'Get away from me,' Manuel said. 'Get to hell away from me.'

He twisted free. Hernandez shrugged his shoulders. Manuel ran towards the bull.

There was the bull standing, heavy, firmly planted.

All right, you bastard! Manuel drew the sword out of the muleta, sighted with the same movement, and flung himself on to the bull. He felt the sword go in all the way. Right up to the guard. Four fingers and his thumb into the bull. The blood was hot on his knuckles, and he was on top of the bull.

The bull lurched with him as he lay on, and seemed to sink; then he was standing clear. He looked at the bull going down slowly over on his side, then suddenly four feet in the air.

Then he gestured at the crowd, his hand warm from the bull blood.

All right, you bastards! He wanted to say something, but he started to cough. It was hot and choking. He looked down for the muleta. He must go over and salute the president. President hell! He was sitting down looking at something. It was the bull. His four feet up. Thick tongue out. Things crawling around on his belly and under his legs. Crawling where the hair was thin. Dead bull. To hell with the bull! To hell with them all! He started to get to his feet and commenced to cough. He sat down again, coughing. Somebody came and pushed him up.

They carried him across the ring to the infirmary, running with him across the sand, standing blocked at the gate as the mules came in, then around under the dark passageway, men grunting as they took him up the stairway, and then laid him down.

The doctor and two men in white were waiting for him. They laid him out on the table. They were cutting away his shirt. Manuel felt tired. His whole chest felt scalding inside. He started to cough and they held something to his mouth. Everybody was very busy.

There was an electric light in his eyes. He shut his eyes.

He heard someone come very heavily up the stairs. Then he did not hear it. Then he heard a noise far off. That was the crowd. Well, somebody would have to kill his other bull.

They had cut away all his shirt. The doctor smiled at him. There was Retana.

'Hello, Retana!' Manuel said. He could not hear his voice.

Retana smiled at him and said something. Manuel could not hear it.

Zurito stood beside the table, bending over where the doctor was working. He was in his picador clothes, without his hat.

Zurito said something to him. Manuel could not hear it.

Zurito was speaking to Retana. One of the men in white smiled and handed Retana a pair of scissors. Retana gave them to Zurito. Zurito said something to Manuel. He could not hear it.

To hell with this operating-table! He'd been on plenty of operating-tables before. He was not going to die. There would be a priest if he was going to die.

Zurito was saying something to him. Holding up the scissors.

That was it. They were going to cut off his coleta. They were going to cut off his pigtail.

Manuel sat up on the operating-table. The doctor stepped back, angry. Someone grabbed him and held him.

'You couldn't do a thing like that, Manos,' he said.

He heard suddenly, clearly, Zurito's voice.

'That's all right,' Zurito said. 'I won't do it. I was joking.'

'I was going good,' Manuel said. 'I didn't have any luck. That was all.'

Manuel lay back. They had put something over his face. It was all familiar. He inhaled deeply. He felt very tired. He was very, very tired. They took the thing away from his face.

'I was going good,' Manuel said weakly. 'I was going great.'

Retana looked at Zurito and started for the door.

'I'll stay here with him,' Zurito said.

Retana shrugged his shoulders.

Manuel opened his eyes and looked at Zurito.

'Wasn't I going good, Manos?' he asked, for confirmation.

'Sure,' said Zurito. 'You were going great.'

The doctor's assistant put the cone over Manuel's face and he inhaled deeply. Zurito stood awkwardly, watching.

IN ANOTHER COUNTRY

In the fall the war was always there, but we did not go to it any more. It was cold in the fall in Milan and the dark came very early. Then the electric lights came on, and it was pleasant along the streets looking in the windows. There was much game hanging outside the shops, and the snow powdered in the fur of the foxes and the wind blew their tails. The deer hung stiff and heavy and empty, and small birds blew in the wind and the wind turned their feathers. It was a cold fall and the wind came down from the mountains.

We were all at the hospital every afternoon, and there were different ways of walking across the town through the dusk to the hospital. Two of the ways were alongside canals, but they were long. Always, though, you crossed a bridge across a canal to enter the hospital. There was a choice of three bridges. On one of them a woman sold roasted chestnuts. It was warm, standing in front of her charcoal fire, and the chestnuts were warm afterward in your pocket. The hospital was very old and very beautiful, and you entered through a gate and walked across a courtyard and out of a gate on the other side. There were usually funerals starting from the courtyard. Beyond the old hospital were the new brick pavilions, and there we met every afternoon and were all very polite and interested in what was the matter, and sat in the machines that were to make so much difference.

The doctor came up to the machine where I was sitting and said: 'What did you like best to do before the war? Did you practise a sport?'

I said: 'Yes, football.'

'Good,' he said. 'You will be able to play football again better than ever.'

My knee did not bend and the leg dropped straight from the knee to the ankle without a calf, and the machine was to bend the knee and make it move as in riding a tricycle. But it did not bend yet, and instead the machine lurched when it came to the bending part. The doctor said: 'That will all pass. You are a fortunate young man. You will play football again like a champion.'

In the next machine was a major who had a little hand like a baby's. He winked at me when the doctor examined his hand, which was between two leather straps that bounced up and down and flapped the stiff fingers, and said: 'And will I too play football, captain-doctor?' He had been a very great fencer and, before the war, the greatest fencer in Italy.

The doctor went to his office in the back room and brought a photograph which showed a hand that had been withered almost as small as the major's, before it had taken a machine course, and after was a little larger. The major held the photograph with his good hand and looked at it very carefully. 'A wound?' he asked.

'An industrial accident,' the doctor said.

'Very interesting, very interesting,' the major said, and handed it back to the doctor.

'You have confidence?'

'No,' said the major.

There were three boys who came each day who were about the same age I was. They were all three from Milan, and one of them was to be a lawyer, and one was to be a painter, and one had intended to be a soldier, and after we were finished with the machines, sometimes we walked back together to the Café Cova, which was next door to the Scala. We walked the short way through the communist quarter because we were four together. The people hated us because we were officers, and from a wine-shop someone would call out, 'A basso gli ufficiali!' as we passed. Another boy who walked with us sometimes and made us five wore a black silk handkerchief across his face because he had no nose then and his face was to be rebuilt. He had gone out to the front from the military academy and been wounded within an hour after he had gone into the front line for the first time. They rebuilt his face, but he came from a very old family and they could never get the nose exactly right. He went to South America and worked in a bank. But this was a long time ago, and then we did not any of us know how it was going to be afterward. We only knew that there was always the war, but that we were not going to it any more.

We all had the same medals, except the boy with the black silk bandage across his face, and he had not been at the front long enough to get any medals. The tall boy with a very pale face who was to be a lawyer had been a lieutenant of Arditi and had three medals of the sort we each had only one of. He had lived a very long time with death and was a little detached. We were all a little detached, and there was nothing that held us together except that we met every afternoon at the hospital. Although, as we walked to the Cova through the tough part of town, walking in the dark, with light and singing coming out of the wine-shops, and sometimes having to walk into the street when the men and women would crowd together on the sidewalk so that we would have had to jostle them to get by, we felt held together by there being something that had happened that they, the people who disliked us, did not understand.

We ourselves all understood the Cova, where it was rich and warm and not too brightly lighted, and noisy and smoky at certain hours, and there were always girls at the tables and the illustrated papers on a rack on the wall. The girls at the Cova were very patriotic, and I found that the most patriotic people in Italy were the café girls – and I believe they are still patriotic.

The boys at first were very polite about my medals and asked me what I had done to get them. I showed them the papers, which were written in very beautiful language and full of *fratellanza* and *abnegazione*, but which really said, with the adjectives removed, that I had been given the medals because I was an American. After that their manner changed a little towards me, although I was their friend against outsiders. I was a friend, but I was never really one of them after they had read the citations, because it had been different with them and they had done very different things to get their medals. I had been wounded, it was true; but we all knew that being wounded, after all, was really an accident. I was never ashamed of the ribbons, though, and sometimes, after the cocktail hour, I would imagine myself having done all the things they had done to get their medals; but walking home at night through the empty streets with the cold wind and all the shops closed, trying to keep near the street lights, I knew that I would never have done such things, and I was very much afraid to die, and often lay in bed at night by myself, afraid to die and wondering how I would be when I went back to the front again.

The three with the medals were like hunting-hawks; and I was not a hawk, although I might seem a hawk to those who have never hunted; they, the three, knew better and so we drifted apart. But I stayed good friends with the boy who had been wounded his first day at the front, because he would never know now how he would have turned out; so he could never be accepted either, and I liked him because I thought perhaps he would not have turned out to be a hawk either.

The major, who had been the great fencer, did not believe in bravery, and spent much time while we sat in the machines correcting my grammar. He had complimented me on how I spoke Italian, and we talked together very easily. One day I had said that Italian seemed such an easy language to me that I could not take a great interest in it; everything was so easy to say. 'Ah, yes,' the major said. 'Why, then, do you not take up the use of grammar?' So we took up the use of grammar, and soon Italian was such a difficult language that I was afraid to talk to him until I had the grammar straight in my mind.

The major came very regularly to the hospital. I do not think he ever missed a day, although I am sure he did not believe in the machines. There was a time when none of us believed in the machines, and one day the major said it was all nonsense. The machines were new then and it was we who were to prove them. It was an idiotic idea, he said, 'a theory, like another.' I had not learned my grammar, and he said I was a stupid impossible disgrace, and he was a fool to have bothered with me. He was a small man and he sat straight up in his chair with his right hand thrust into the machine and looked straight ahead at the wall while the straps thumped up and down with his fingers in them.

'What will you do when the war is over if it is over?' he asked me. 'Speak grammatically!'

'I will go to the States.'

'Are you married?'

'No, but I hope to be.'

'The more of a fool you are,' he said. He seemed very angry. 'A man must not marry.'

'Why, signor maggiore?'

'Don't call me "signor maggiore".'

'Why must not a man marry?'

'He cannot marry. He cannot marry,' he said angrily. 'If he is to lose everything, he should not place himself in a position to lose that. He should not place himself in a position to lose. He should find things he cannot lose.'

He spoke very angrily and bitterly, and looked straight ahead while he talked.

'But why should he necessarily lose it?'

'He'll lose it,' the major said. He was looking at the wall. Then he looked down at the machine and jerked his little hand out from between the straps and slapped it hard against his thigh. 'He'll lose it,' he almost shouted. 'Don't argue with me!' Then he called to the attendant who ran the machines. 'Come and turn this damned thing off.'

He went back into the other room for the light treatment and the massage. Then I heard him ask the doctor if he might use his telephone and he shut the door. When he came back into the room, I was sitting in another machine. He was wearing his cape and had his cap on, and he came directly towards my machine and put his arm on my shoulder.

'I am so sorry,' he said, and patted me on the shoulder with his good hand. 'I would not be rude. My wife has just died. You must forgive me.'

'Oh –' I said, feeling sick for him. 'I am *so* sorry.'

He stood there biting his lower lip. 'It is very difficult,' he said. 'I cannot resign myself.'

He looked straight past me and out through the window. Then he began to cry. 'I am utterly unable to resign myself,' he said and choked. And then crying, his head up, looking at nothing, carrying himself straight and soldierly, with tears on both his cheeks and biting his lips, he walked past the machines and out of the door.

The doctor told me that the major's wife, who was very young and whom he had not married until he was definitely invalided out of the war, had died of pneumonia. She had been sick only a few days. No one expected her to die. The major did not come to the hospital for three days. Then he came at the usual hour, wearing a black band on the sleeve of his uniform. When he came back, there were large framed photographs around the wall, of all sorts of wounds before and after they had been cured by the machines. In front of the machine the major used were three photographs of hands like his that were completely restored. I do not know where the doctor got them. I always understood we were the first to use the machines. The photographs did not make much difference to the major because he only looked out of the window.

HILLS LIKE WHITE ELEPHANTS

The hills across the valley of the Ebro were long and white. On this side there was no shade and no trees and the station was between two lines of rails in the sun. Close against the side of the station there was the warm shadow of the building and a curtain, made of strings of bamboo beads, hung across the open door into the bar, to keep out flies. The American and the girl with him sat at a table in the shade, outside the building. It was very hot and the express from Barcelona would come in forty minutes. It stopped at this junction for two minutes and went on to Madrid.

'What should we drink?' the girl asked. She had taken off her hat and put it on the table.

'It's pretty hot,' the man said.

'Let's drink beer.'

'Dos cervezas,' the man said into the curtain.

'Big ones?' a woman asked from the doorway.

'Yes. Two big ones.'

The woman brought two glasses of beer and two felt pads. She put the felt pads and the beer glasses on the table and looked at the man and the girl. The girl was looking off at the line of hills. They were white in the sun and the country was brown and dry.

'They look like white elephants,' she said.

'I've never seen one.' The man drank his beer.

'No, you wouldn't have.'

'I might have,' the man said. 'Just because you say I wouldn't have doesn't prove anything.'

The girl looked at the bead curtain. 'They've painted something on it,' she said. 'What does it say?'

'Anis del Toro. It's a drink.'

'Could we try it?'

The man called 'Listen' through the curtain.

The woman came out from the bar.

'Four reales.'

44

'We want two Anis del Toros.'

'With water?'

'Do you want it with water?'

'I don't know,' the girl said. 'Is it good with water?'

'It's all right.'

'You want them with water?' asked the woman.

'Yes, with water.'

'It tastes like licorice,' the girl said and put the glass down.

'That's the way with everything.'

'Yes,' said the girl. 'Everything tastes of licorice. Especially all the things you've waited so long for, like absinthe.'

'Oh, cut it out.'

'You started it,' the girl said. 'I was being amused. I was having a fine time.'

'Well, let's try and have a fine time.'

'All right. I was trying. I said the mountains looked like white elephants. Wasn't that bright?'

'That was bright.'

'I wanted to try this new drink. That's all we do, isn't it – look at things and try new drinks?'

'I guess so.'

The girl looked across at the hills.

'They're lovely hills,' she said. 'They don't really look like white elephants. I just meant the colouring of their skin through the trees.'

'Should we have another drink?'

'All right.'

The warm wind blew the bead curtain against the table.

'The beer's nice and cool,' the man said.

'It's lovely,' the girl said.

'It's really an awfully simple operation, Jig,' the man said. 'It's not really an operation at all.'

The girl looked at the ground the table legs rested on.

'I know you wouldn't mind it, Jig. It's really not anything. It's just to let the air in.'

The girl did not say anything.

'I'll go with you and I'll stay with you all the time. They just let the air in and then it's all perfectly natural.'

'Then what will we do afterwards?'

'We'll be fine afterwards. Just like we were before.'

'What makes you think so?'

'That's the only thing that bothers us. It's the only thing that's made us unhappy.'

The girl looked at the bead curtain, put her hand out and took hold of two of the strings of beads.

'And you think then we'll be all right and be happy.'

'I know we will. You don't have to be afraid. I've known lots of people that have done it.'

'So have I,' said the girl. 'And afterward they were all so happy.'

'Well,' the man said, 'if you don't want to you don't have to. I wouldn't have you do it if you didn't want to. But I know it's perfectly simple.'

'And you really want to?'

'I think it's the best thing to do. But I don't want you to do it if you don't really want to.'

'And if I do it you'll be happy and things will be like they were and you'll love me?'

'I love you now. You know I love you.'

'I know. But if I do it, then it will be nice again if I say things are like white elephants, and you'll like it?'

'I'll love it. I love it now but I just can't think about it. You know how I get when I worry.'

'If I do it you won't ever worry?'

'I won't worry about that because it's perfectly simple.'

'Then I'll do it. Because I don't care about me.'

'What do you mean?'

'I don't care about me.'

'Well, I care about you.'

'Oh, yes. But I don't care about me. And I'll do it and then everything will be fine.'

'I don't want you to do it if you feel that way.'

The girl stood up and walked to the end of the station. Across, on the other side, were fields of grain and trees along the banks of the Ebro. Far away, beyond the river, were mountains. The shadow of a cloud moved across the field of grain and she saw the river through the trees.

'And we could have all this,' she said. 'And we could have

everything and every day we make it more impossible.'

'What did you say?'

'I said we could have everything.'

'We can have everything.'

'No, we can't.'

'We can have the whole world.'

'No, we can't.'

'We can go everywhere.'

'No, we can't. It isn't ours any more.'

'It's ours.'

'No, it isn't. And once they take it away, you never get it back.'

'But they haven't taken it away.'

'We'll wait and see.'

'Come on back in the shade,' he said. 'You mustn't feel that way.'

'I don't feel any way,' the girl said. 'I just know things.'

'I don't want you to do anything that you don't want to do –'

'Nor that isn't good for me,' she said. 'I know. Could we have another beer?'

'All right. But you've got to realize –'

'I realize,' the girl said. 'Can't we maybe stop talking?'

They sat down at the table and the girl looked across at the hills on the dry side of the valley and the man looked at her and at the table.

'You've got to realize,' he said, 'that I don't want you to do it if you don't want to. I'm perfectly willing to go through with it if it means anything to you.'

'Doesn't it mean anything to you? We could get along.'

'Of course it does. But I don't want anybody but you. I don't want anyone else. And I know it's perfectly simple.'

'Yes, you know it's perfectly simple.'

'It's all right for you to say that, but I do know it.'

'Would you do something for me now?'

'I'd do anything for you.'

'Would you please please please please please please please stop talking?'

He did not say anything but looked at the bags against the

wall of the station. There were labels on them from all the hotels where they had spent nights.

'But I don't want you to,' he said, 'I don't care anything about it.'

'I'll scream,' the girl said.

The woman came out through the curtains with two glasses of beer and put them down on the damp felt pads. 'The train comes in five minutes,' she said.

'What did she say?' asked the girl.

'That the train is coming in five minutes.'

The girl smiled brightly at the woman, to thank her.

'I'd better take the bags over to the other side of the station,' the man said. She smiled at him.

'All right. Then come back and we'll finish the beer.'

He picked up the two heavy bags and carried them around the station to the other tracks. He looked up the tracks but could not see the train. Coming back, he walked through the bar-room, where people waiting for the train were drinking. He drank an Anis at the bar and looked at the people. They were all waiting reasonably for the train. He went out through the bead curtain. She was sitting at the table and smiled at him.

'Do you feel better?' he asked.

'I feel fine,' she said. 'There's nothing wrong with me. I feel fine.'

The door of Henry's lunch-room opened and two men came in. They sat down at the counter.

'What's yours?' George asked them.

'I don't know,' one of the men said. 'What do you want to eat, Al?'

'I don't know,' said Al. 'I don't know what I want to eat.'

Outside it was getting dark. The street-light came on outside the window. The two men at the counter read the menu. From the other end of the counter Nick Adams watched them. He had been talking to George when they came in.

'I'll have a roast pork tenderloin with apple sauce and mashed potatoes,' the first man said.

'It isn't ready yet.'

'What the hell do you put it on the card for?'

'That's the dinner,' George explained. 'You can get that at six o'clock.'

George looked at the clock on the wall behind the counter.

'It's five o'clock.'

'The clock says twenty minutes past five,' the second man said.

'It's twenty minutes fast.'

'Oh, to hell with the clock,' the first man said. 'What have you got to eat?'

'I can give you any kind of sandwiches,' George said. 'You can have ham and eggs, bacon and eggs, liver and bacon, or a steak.'

'Give me chicken croquettes with green peas and cream sauce and mashed potatoes.'

'That's the dinner.'

'Everything we want's the dinner, eh? That's the way you work it.'

'I can give you ham and eggs, bacon and eggs, liver –'

'I'll take ham and eggs,' the man called Al said. He wore a derby hat and a black overcoat buttoned across the chest. His face was small and white and he had tight lips. He wore a silk muffler and gloves.

'Give me bacon and eggs,' said the other man. He was about the same size as Al. Their faces were different, but they were dressed like twins. Both wore overcoats too tight for them. They sat leaning forward, their elbows on the counter.

'Got anything to drink?' Al asked.

'Silver beer, bevo, ginger-ale,' George said.

'I mean you got anything to *drink*?'

'Just those I said.'

'This is a hot town,' said the other. 'What do they call it?'

'Summit.'

'Ever hear of it?' Al asked his friend.

'No,' said the friend.

'What do you do here nights?' Al asked.

'They eat the dinner,' his friend said. 'They all come here and eat the big dinner.'

'That's right,' George said.

'So you think that's right?' Al asked George.

'Sure.'

'You're a pretty bright boy, aren't you?'

'Sure,' said George.

'Well, you're not,' said the other little man. 'Is he, Al?'

'He's dumb,' said Al. He turned to Nick. 'What's your name?'

'Adams.'

'Another bright boy,' Al said. 'Ain't he a bright boy, Max?'

'The town's full of bright boys,' Max said.

George put the two platters, one of ham and eggs, the other of bacon and eggs, on the counter. He set down two side-dishes of fried potatoes and closed the wicket into the kitchen.

'Which is yours?' he asked Al.

'Don't you remember?'

'Ham and eggs.'

'Just a bright boy,' Max said. He leaned forward and took the ham and eggs. Both men ate with their gloves on. George watched them eat.

'What are *you* looking at?' Max looked at George.

'Nothing.'

'The hell you were. You were looking at me.'

'Maybe the boy meant it for a joke, Max,' Al said.

George laughed.

'*You* don't have to laugh,' Max said to him. '*You* don't have to laugh at all, see?'

'All right,' said George.

'So he thinks it's all right,' Max turned to Al. 'He thinks it's all right. That's a good one.'

'Oh, he's a thinker,' Al said. They went on eating.

'What's the bright boy's name down the counter?' Al asked Max.

'Hey, bright boy,' Max said to Nick. 'You go around on the other side of the counter with your boy friend.'

'What's the idea?' Nick asked.

'There isn't any idea.'

'You better go around, bright boy,' Al said. Nick went around behind the counter.

'What's the idea?' George asked.

'None of your damn business,' Al said. 'Who's out in the kitchen?'

'The nigger.'

'What do you mean the nigger?'

'The nigger that cooks.'

'Tell him to come in.'

'What's the idea?'

'Tell him to come in.'

'Where do you think you are?'

'We know damn well where we are,' the man called Max said. 'Do we look silly?'

'You talk silly,' Al said to him. 'What the hell do you argue with this kid for? Listen,' he said to George, 'tell the nigger to come out here.'

'What are you going to do to him?'

'Nothing. Use your head, bright boy. What would we do to a nigger?'

George opened the slip that opened back into the kitchen. 'Sam,' he called. 'Come in here a minute.'

The door to the kitchen opened and the nigger came in.

51

'What was it?' he asked. The two men at the counter took a look at him.

'All right, nigger. You stand right there,' Al said.

Sam, the nigger, standing in his apron, looked at the two men sitting at the counter. 'Yes, sir,' he said. Al got down from his stool.

'I'm going back to the kitchen with the nigger and bright boy,' he said. 'Go back to the kitchen, nigger. You go with him, bright boy.' The little man walked after Nick and Sam, the cook, back into the kitchen. The door shut after them. The man called Max sat at the counter opposite George. He didn't look at George but looked in the mirror that ran along back of the counter. Henry's had been made over from a saloon into a lunch-counter.

'Well, bright boy,' Max said, looking into the mirror, 'why don't you say something?'

'What's it all about?'

'Hey, Al,' Max called, 'bright boy wants to know what it's all about.'

'Why don't you tell him?' Al's voice came from the kitchen.

'What do you think it's all about?'

'I don't know.'

'What do you think?'

Max looked into the mirror all the time he was talking.

'I wouldn't say.'

'Hey, Al, bright boy says he wouldn't say what he thinks it's all about.'

'I can hear you, all right,' Al said from the kitchen. He had propped open the slit that dishes passed through into the kitchen with a catsup bottle. 'Listen, bright boy,' he said from the kitchen to George. 'Stand a little further along the bar. You move a little to the left, Max.' He was like a photographer arranging for a group picture.

'Talk to me, bright boy.' Max said. 'What do you think's going to happen?'

George did not say anything.

'I'll tell you,' Max said. 'We're going to kill a Swede. Do you know a big Swede named Ole Andreson?'

'Yes.'

'He comes here to eat every night, don't he?'

'Sometimes he comes here.'

'He comes here at six o'clock, don't he?'

'If he comes.'

'We know all that, bright boy,' Max said. 'Talk about something else. Ever go to the movies?'

'Once in a while.'

'You ought to go to the movies more. The movies are fine for a bright boy like you.'

'What are you going to kill Ole Andreson for? What did he ever do to you?'

'He never had a chance to do anything to us. He never even seen us.'

'And he's only going to see us once,' Al said from the kitchen.

'What are you going to kill him for, then?' George asked.

'We're killing him for a friend. Just to oblige a friend, bright boy.'

'Shut up,' said Al from the kitchen. 'You talk too goddam much.'

'Well, I got to keep bright boy amused. Don't I, bright boy?'

'You talk too damn much,' Al said. 'The nigger and my bright boy are amused by themselves. I got them tied up like a couple of girl friends in the convent.'

'I suppose you were in a convent.'

'You never know.'

'You were in a kosher convent. That's where you were.'

George looked up at the clock.

'If anybody comes in you tell them the cook is off, and if they keep after it, you tell them you'll go back and cook yourself. Do you get that, bright boy?'

'All right,' George said. 'What you going to do with us afterwards?'

'That'll depend,' Max said. 'That's one of those things you never know at the time.'

George looked up at the clock. It was a quarter past six. The door from the street opened. A street-car motorman came in.

'Hello, George,' he said. 'Can I get supper?'

'Sam's gone out,' George said. 'He'll be back in about half-an-hour.'

'I'd better go up the street,' the motorman said. George looked at the clock. It was twenty minutes past six.

'That was nice, bright boy,' Max said. 'You're a regular little gentleman.'

'He knew I'd blow his head off,' Al said from the kitchen.

'No,' said Max. 'It ain't that. Bright boy is nice. He's a nice boy. I like him.'

At six-fifty-five George said: 'He's not coming.'

Two other people had been in the lunch-room. Once George had gone out to the kitchen and made a ham-and-egg sandwich 'to go' that a man wanted to take with him. Inside the kitchen he saw Al, his derby hat tipped back, sitting on a stool beside the wicket with the muzzle of a sawed-off shotgun resting on the ledge. Nick and the cook were back to back in the corner, a towel tied in each of their mouths. George had cooked the sandwich, wrapped it up in oiled paper, put it in a bag, brought it in, and the man had paid for it and gone out.

'Bright boy can do everything,' Max said. 'He can cook and everything. You'd make some girl a nice wife, bright boy.'

'Yes?' George said. 'Your friend, Ole Andreson, isn't going to come.'

'We'll give him ten minutes,' Max said.

Max watched the mirror and the clock. The hands of the clock marked seven o'clock, and then five minutes past seven.

'Come on, Al,' said Max. 'We better go. He's not coming.'

'Better give him five minutes,' Al said from the kitchen.

In the five minutes a man came in, and George explained that the cook was sick.

'Why the hell don't you get another cook?' the man asked. 'Aren't you running a lunch-counter?' He went out.

'Come on, Al,' Max said.

'What about the two bright boys and the nigger?'

'They're all right.'

'You think so?'

'Sure. We're through with it.'

'I don't like it,' said Al. 'It's sloppy. You talk too much.'

54

'Oh, what the hell,' said Max. 'We got to keep amused, haven't we?'

'You talk too much, all the same,' Al said. He came out from the kitchen. The cut-off barrels of the shotgun made a slight bulge under the waist of his too tight-fitting overcoat. He straightened his coat with his gloved hands.

'So long, bright boy,' he said to George. 'You got a lot of luck.'

'That's the truth,' Max said. 'You ought to play the races, bright boy.'

The two of them went out the door. George watched them, through the window, pass under the arc-light and cross the street. In their tight overcoats and derby hats they looked like a vaudeville team. George went back through the swinging-door into the kitchen and untied Nick and the cook.

'I don't want any more of that,' said Sam, the cook. 'I don't want any more of that.'

Nick stood up. He had never had a towel in his mouth before.

'Say,' he said. 'What the hell?' He was trying to swagger it off.

'They were going to kill Ole Andreson,' George said. 'They were going to shoot him when he came in to eat.'

'Ole Andreson?'

'Sure.'

The cook felt the corners of his mouth with his thumbs.

'They all gone?' he asked.

'Yeah,' said George. 'They're gone now.'

'I don't like it,' said the cook. 'I don't like any of it at all.'

'Listen,' George said to Nick. 'You better go see Ole Andreson.'

'All right.'

'You better not have anything to do with it at all,' Sam, the cook, said. 'You better stay way out of it.'

'Don't go if you don't want to,' George said.

'Mixing up in this ain't going to get you anywhere,' the cook said. 'You stay out of it.'

'I'll go see him,' Nick said to George. 'Where does he live?'

The cook turned away.

'Little boys always know what they want to do,' he said.

'He lives up at Hirsch's rooming-house,' George said to Nick.

'I'll go up there.'

Outside, the arc-light shone through the bare branches of a tree. Nick walked up the street beside the car-tracks and turned at the next arc-light down a side-street. Three houses up the street was Hirsch's rooming-house. Nick walked up the two steps and pushed the bell. A woman came to the door.

'Is Ole Andreson here?'

'Do you want to see him?'

'Yes, if he's in.'

Nick followed the woman up a flight of stairs and back to the end of the corridor. She knocked on the door.

'Who is it?'

'It's somebody to see you, Mr Andreson,' the woman said.

'It's Nick Adams.'

'Come in.'

Nick opened the door and went into the room. Ole Andreson was lying on the bed with all his clothes on. He had been a heavyweight prizefighter and he was too long for the bed. He lay with his head on two pillows. He did not look at Nick.

'What was it?' he asked.

'I was up at Henry's,' Nick said, 'and two fellows came in and tied up me and the cook, and they said they were going to kill you.'

It sounded silly when he said it. Ole Andreson said nothing.

'They put us out in the kitchen,' Nick went on. 'They were going to shoot you when you came in to supper.'

Ole Andreson looked at the wall and did not say anything.

'George thought I better come and tell you about it.'

'There isn't anything I can do about it,' Ole Andreson said.

'I'll tell you what they were like.'

'I don't want to know what they were like,' Ole Andreson said. He looked at the wall. 'Thanks for coming to tell me about it.'

'That's all right.'

Nick looked at the big man lying on the bed.

'Don't you want me to go and see the police?'

'No,' Ole Andreson said. 'That wouldn't do any good.'

'Isn't there something I could do?'

'No. There ain't anything to do.'

'Maybe it was just a bluff.'

'No. It ain't just a bluff.'

Ole Andreson rolled over towards the wall.

'The only thing is,' he said, talking towards the wall, 'I just can't make up my mind to go out. I been in here all day.'

'Couldn't you get out of town?'

'No,' Ole Andreson said. 'I'm through with all that running around.'

He looked at the wall.

'There ain't anything to do now.'

'Couldn't you fix it up some way?'

'No. I got in wrong.' He talked in the same flat voice. 'There ain't anything to do. After a while I'll make up my mind to go out.'

'I better go back and see George,' Nick said.

'So long,' said Ole Andreson. He did not look towards Nick. 'Thanks for coming around.'

Nick went out. As he shut the door he saw Ole Andreson with all his clothes on, lying on the bed looking at the wall.

'He's been in his room all day,' the landlady said downstairs. 'I guess he don't feel well. I said to him: "Mr Andreson, you ought to go out and take a walk on a nice fall day like this," but he didn't feel like it.'

'He doesn't want to go out.'

'I'm sorry he don't feel well,' the woman said. 'He's an awfully nice man. He was in the ring, you know.'

'I know it.'

'You'd never know it except for the way his face is,' the woman said. They stood talking just inside the street door. 'He's just as gentle.'

'Well, good-night, Mrs Hirsch,' Nick said.

'I'm not Mrs Hirsch,' the woman said. 'She owns the place. I just look after it for her. I'm Mrs Bell.'

'Well, good-night, Mrs Bell,' Nick said.

'Good-night,' the woman said.

Nick walked up the dark street to the corner under the

arc-light, and then along the car-tracks to Henry's eating-house. George was inside, back of the counter.

'Did you see Ole?'

'Yes,' said Nick. 'He's in his room and he won't go out.'

The cook opened the door from the kitchen when he heard Nick's voice.

'I don't even listen to it,' he said and shut the door.

'Did you tell him about it?' George asked.

'Sure. I told him, but he knows what it's all about.'

'What's he going to do?'

'Nothing.'

'They'll kill him.'

'I guess they will.'

'He must have got mixed up in something in Chicago.'

'I guess so,' said Nick.

'It's a hell of a thing.'

'It's an awful thing,' Nick said.

They did not say anything. George reached down for a towel and wiped the counter.

'I wonder what he did?' Nick said.

'Double-crossed somebody. That's what they kill them for.'

'I'm going to get out of this town,' Nick said.

'Yes,' said George. 'That's a good thing to do.'

'I can't stand to think about him waiting in the room and knowing he's going to get it. It's too damned awful.'

'Well,' said George, 'you better not think about it.'

The road of the pass was hard and smooth and not yet dusty in the early morning. Below were the hills with oak and chestnut trees, and far away below was the sea. On the other side were snowy mountains.

We came down from the pass through wooded country. There were bags of charcoal piled beside the road, and through the trees we saw charcoal-burners' huts. It was Sunday and the road, rising and falling, but always dropping away from the altitude of the pass, went through the scrub woods and through villages.

Outside the villages there were fields with vines. The fields were brown and the vines coarse and thick. The houses were white, and in the streets the men, in their Sunday clothes, were playing bowls. Against the walls of some of the houses there were pear trees, their branches candelabraed against the white walls. The pear trees had been sprayed, and the walls of the houses were stained a metallic blue-green by the spray vapour. There were small clearings around the villages where the vines grew, and then the woods.

In a village, twenty kilometres above Spezia, there was a crowd in the square, and a young man carrying a suitcase came up to the car and asked us to take him in to Spezia.

'There are only two places, and they are occupied,' I said. We had an old Ford coupé.

'I will ride on the outside.'

'You will be uncomfortable.'

'That makes nothing. I must go to Spezia.'

'Should we take him?' I asked Guy.

'He seems to be going anyway,' Guy said. The young man handed in a parcel through the window.

'Look after this,' he said. Two men tied his suitcase on the back of the car, above our suitcases. He shook hands with everyone, explained that to a Fascist and a man as used to travelling as himself there was no discomfort, and climbed up on the running board on the left-hand side of the car, holding on inside, his right arm through the open window.

'You can start,' he said. The crowd waved. He waved with his free hand.

'What did he say?' Guy asked me.

'That we could start.'

'Isn't he nice?' Guy said.

The road followed a river. Across the river were mountains. The sun was taking the frost out of the grass. It was bright and cold and the air came cold through the open wind-shield.

'How do you think he likes it out there?' Guy was looking up the road. His view out of his side of the car was blocked by our guest. The young man projected from the side of the car like the figurehead of a ship. He had turned his coat collar up and pulled his hat down and his nose looked cold in the wind.

'Maybe he'll get enough of it,' Guy said. 'That's the side our bum tyre's on.'

'Oh, he'd leave us if we blew out,' I said. 'He wouldn't get his travelling clothes dirty.'

'Well, I don't mind him,' Guy said – 'except the way he leans out on the turns.'

The woods were gone; the road had left the river to climb; the radiator was boiling; the young man looked annoyedly and suspiciously at the steam and rusty water; the engine was grinding, with both Guy's feet on the first-speed pedal, up and up, back and forth, and up, and, finally, out level. The grinding stopped, and in the new quiet there was a great churning bubbling in the radiator. We were at the top of the last range above Spezia and the sea. The road descended with short, barely rounded turns. Our guest hung out on the turns and nearly pulled the top-heavy car over.

'You can't tell him not to,' I said to Guy. 'It's his sense of self-preservation.'

'The great Italian sense.'

'The greatest Italian sense.'

We came down around curves, through deep dust, the dust powdering the olive trees. Spezia spread below along the sea. The road flattened outside the town. Our guest put his head in the window.

'I want to stop.'

'Stop it,' I said to Guy.

We slowed up, at the side of the road. The young man got down, went to the back of the car and untied the suitcase.

'I stop here, so you won't get into trouble carrying passengers,' he said. 'My package.'

I handed him the package. He reached in his pocket.

'How much do I owe you?'

'Nothing.'

'Why not?'

'I don't know,' I said.

'Then thanks,' the young man said, not 'thank you,' or 'thank you very much,' or 'thank you a thousand times,' all of which you formerly said in Italy to a man when he handed you a timetable or explained about a direction. The young man uttered the lowest form of the word 'thanks' and looked after us suspiciously as Guy started the car. I waved my hand at him. He was too dignified to reply. We went on into Spezia.

'That's a young man that will go a long way in Italy,' I said to Guy.

'Well,' said Guy, 'he went twenty kilometres with us.'

A MEAL IN SPEZIA

We came into Spezia looking for a place to eat. The street was wide and the houses high and yellow. We followed the tramtrack into the centre of town. On the walls of the houses were stencilled eye-bugging portraits of Mussolini, with hand-painted 'vivas', the double V in black paint with drippings of paint down the wall. Side-streets went down to the harbour. It was bright and the people were all out for Sunday. The stone paving had been sprinkled and there were damp stretches in the dust. We went close to the curb to avoid a tram.

'Let's eat somewhere simple,' Guy said.

We stopped opposite two restaurant signs. We were standing across the street and I was buying the papers. The two restaurants were side by side. A woman standing in the doorway of one smiled at us and we crossed the street and went in.

It was dark inside and at the back of the room three girls were sitting at a table with an old woman. Across from us, at another table, sat a sailor. He sat there neither eating nor drinking. Further back, a young man in a blue suit was writing at a table. His hair was pomaded and shining and he was very smartly dressed and clean-cut looking.

The light came through the doorway, and through the window where vegetables, fruit, steaks, and chops were arranged in a show-case. A girl came and took our order and another girl stood in the doorway. We noticed that she wore nothing under her house dress. The girl who took our order put her arm around Guy's neck while we were looking at the menu. There were three girls in all, and they all took turns going and standing in the doorway. The old woman at the table in the back of the room spoke to them and they sat down again with her.

There was no doorway leading from the room except into the kitchen. A curtain hung over it. The girl who had taken our order came in from the kitchen with spaghetti. She put it on the table and brought a bottle of red wine and sat down at the table.

'Well,' I said to Guy, 'you wanted to eat at some place simple.'

'This isn't simple. This is complicated.'

'What do you say?' asked the girl. 'Are you Germans?'

'South Germans,' I said. 'The South Germans are a gentle, lovable people.'

'Don't understand,' she said.

'What's the mechanics of this place?' Guy asked. 'Do I have to let her put her arm around my neck?'

'Certainly,' I said. 'Mussolini has abolished the brothels. This is a restaurant.'

The girl wore a one-piece dress. She leaned forward against the table and put her hands on her breasts and smiled. She smiled better on one side than on the other and turned the good side towards us. The charm of the good side had been enhanced by some event which had smoothed the other side of her nose in, as warm wax can be smoothed. Her nose, however, did not look like warm wax. It was very cold and firmed, only smoothed in. 'You like me?' she asked Guy.

'He adores you,' I said. 'But he doesn't speak Italian.'

'Ich spreche Deutsch,' she said, and stroked Guy's hair.

'Speak to the lady in your native tongue, Guy.'

'Where do you come from?' asked the lady.

'Potsdam.'

'And you will stay here now for a little while?'

'In this so dear Spezia?' I asked.

'Tell her we have to go,' said Guy. 'Tell her we are very ill, and have no money.'

'My friend is a misogynist,' I said, 'an old German misogynist.'

'Tell him I love him.'

I told him.

'Will you shut your mouth and get us out of here?' Guy said. The lady had placed another arm around his neck. 'Tell him he is mine,' she said. I told him.

'Will you get us out of here?'

'You are quarrelling,' the lady said. 'You do not love one another.'

'We are Germans,' I said proudly, 'old South Germans.'

'Tell him he is a beautiful boy,' the lady said. Guy is thirty-eight and takes some pride in the fact that he is taken for a travelling salesman in France. 'You are a beautiful boy,' I said.

'Who says so?' Guy asked, 'you or her?'

'She does. I'm just your interpreter. Isn't that what you got me in on this trip for?'

'I'm glad it's her,' said Guy. 'I don't want to have to leave you here too.'

'I don't know. Spezia's a lovely place.'

'Spezia,' the lady said. 'You are talking about Spezia.'

'Lovely place,' I said.

'It is my country,' she said. 'Spezia is my home and Italy is my country.'

'She says that Italy is her country.'

'Tell her it looks like her country,' Guy said.

'What have you for dessert?' I asked.

'Fruit,' she said. 'We have bananas.'

'Bananas are all right,' Guy said. 'They've got skins on.'

'Oh, he takes bananas,' the lady said. She embraced Guy.

'What does she say?' he asked, keeping his face out of her way.

'She is pleased because you take bananas.'

'Tell her I don't take bananas.'

'The Signor does not take bananas.'

'Ah,' said the lady, crestfallen, 'he doesn't take bananas.'

'Tell her I take a cold bath every morning,' Guy said.

'The Signor takes a cold bath every morning.'

'No understand,' the lady said.

Across from us, the property sailor had not moved. No one in the place paid any attention to him.

'We want the bill,' I said.

'Oh, no. You must stay.'

'Listen,' the clean-cut young man said from the table where he was writing, 'let them go. These two are worth nothing.'

The lady took my hand. 'You won't stay? You won't ask him to stay?'

'We have to go,' I said. 'We have to get to Pisa, or if possible, Firenze, tonight. We can amuse ourselves in those cities at the end of the day. It is now the day. In the day we must cover distance.'

'To stay a little while is nice.'

'To travel is necessary during the light of day.'

'Listen,' the clean-cut young man said. 'Don't bother to talk with these two. I tell you they are worth nothing and I know.'

'Bring us the bill,' I said. She brought the bill from the old woman and went back and sat at the table. Another girl came in from the kitchen. She walked the length of the room and stood in the doorway.

'Don't bother with these two,' the clean-cut young man said in a wearied voice. 'Come and eat. They are worth nothing.'

We paid the bill and stood up. All the girls, the old woman, and the clean-cut young man sat down at the table together. The property sailor sat with his head in his hands. No one had spoken to him all the time we were at lunch. The girl brought us our change that the old woman counted out for her and went back to her place at the table. We left a tip on the table

64

and went out. When we were seated in the car ready to start, the girl came out and stood in the door. We started and I waved to her. She did not wave, but stood there looking after us.

AFTER THE RAIN

It was raining hard when we passed through the suburbs of Genoa and, even going very slowly behind the tram-cars and the motor trucks, liquid mud splashed on to the sidewalks, so that people stepped into doorways as they saw us coming. In San Pier d'Arena, the industrial suburb outside of Genoa, there is a wide street with two car-tracks and we drove down the centre to avoid sending the mud on to the men going home from work. On our left was the Mediterranean. There was a big sea running and waves broke and the wind blew the spray against the car. A river-bed that, when we had passed, going into Italy, had been wide, stony and dry, was running brown, and up to the banks. The brown water discoloured the sea and as the waves thinned and cleared in breaking, the light came through the yellow water and the crests, detached by the wind, blew across the road.

A big car passed us, going fast, and a sheet of muddy water rose up and over our wind-shield and radiator. The automatic wind-shield cleaner moved back and forth, spreading the film over the glass. We stopped and ate lunch at Sestri. There was no heat in the restaurant and we kept our hats and coats on. We could see the car outside, through the window. It was covered with mud and was stopped beside some boats that had been pulled up beyond the waves. In the restaurant you could see your breath.

The *pasta asciuta* was good; the wine tasted of alum, and we poured water in it. Afterwards the waiter brought beefsteak and fried potatoes. A man and a woman sat at the far end of the restaurant. He was middle-aged and she was young and wore black. All during the meal she would blow out her breath in the cold damp air. The man would look at it and shake his head. They ate without talking and the man held her hand under the table. She was good-looking and they seemed very sad. They had a travelling-bag with them.

We had the papers and I read the account of the Shanghai fighting aloud to Guy. After the meal, he left with the waiter in search for a place which did not exist in the restaurant, and I cleaned off the wind-shield, the lights and the licence plates with a rag. Guy came back and we backed the car out and started. The waiter had taken him across the road and into an old house. The people in the house were suspicious and the waiter had remained with Guy to see nothing was stolen.

'Although I don't know how, me not being a plumber, they expected me to steal anything,' Guy said.

As we came up on a headland beyond the town, the wind struck the car and nearly tipped it over.

'It's good, it blows us away from the sea,' Guy said.

'Well,' I said, 'they drowned Shelley somewhere along here.'

'That was down by Viareggio,' Guy said. 'Do you remember what we came to this country for?'

'Yes,' I said, 'but we didn't get it.'

'We'll be out of it tonight.'

'If we can get past Ventimiglia.'

'We'll see. I don't like to drive this coast at night.' It was early afternoon and the sun was out. Below, the sea was blue with whitecaps running towards Savona. Back beyond the cape the brown and blue waters joined. Out ahead of us, a tramp steamer was going up the coast.

'Can you still see Genoa?' Guy asked.

'Oh, yes.'

'That next big cape ought to put it out of sight.'

'We'll see it a long time yet. I can still see Portofino Cape behind it.'

Finally we could not see Genoa. I looked back as we came out and there was only the sea, and below in the bay, a line of beach with fishing-boats and above, on the side of a hill, a town and then capes far down the coast.

'It's gone now,' I said to Guy.

'Oh, it's been gone a long time now.'

'But we couldn't be sure till we got way out.'

There was a sign with a picture of an S-turn and Svolta Pericolosa. The road curved around the headland and the wind blew through the crack in the wind-shield. Below the cape was a flat stretch beside the sea. The wind had dried the mud and the wheels were beginning to lift dust. On the flat road we passed a Fascist riding a bicycle, a heavy revolver in a holster on his back. He held the middle of the road on his bicycle and we turned out for him. He looked up at us as we passed. Ahead there was a railway crossing, and as we came towards it the gates went down.

As we waited, the Fascist came up on his bicycle. The train went by and Guy started the engine.

'Wait,' the bicycle man shouted from behind the car. 'Your number's dirty.'

I got out with a rag. The number had been cleaned at lunch.

'You can read it,' I said.

'You think so?'

'Read it.'

'I cannot read it. It is dirty.'

I wiped it off with the rag.

'How's that?'

'Twenty-five lire.'

'What?' I said. 'You could have read it. It's only dirty from the state of the roads.'

'You don't like Italian roads?'

'They are dirty.'

'Fifty lire.' He spat in the road. 'Your car is dirty and you are dirty too.'

'Good. And give me a receipt with your name.'

He took out a receipt book, made in duplicate, and perforated, so one side could be given to the customer, and the other side filled in and kept as a stub. There was no carbon to record what the customer's ticket said.

'Give me fifty lire.'

He wrote in indelible pencil, tore out the slip and handed it to me. I read it.

'This is for twenty-five lire.'

'A mistake,' he said, and changed the twenty-five to fifty.

'And now the other side. Make it fifty in the part you keep.'

He smiled a beautiful Italian smile and wrote something on the receipt stub, holding it so I could not see.

'Go on,' he said, 'before your number gets dirty again.'

We drove for two hours after it was dark and slept in Mentone that night. It seemed very cheerful and clean and sane and lovely. We had driven from Ventimiglia to Pisa and Florence, across the Romagna to Rimini, back through Forli, Imola, Bologna, Parma, Piacenza and Genoa, to Ventimiglia again. The whole trip had only taken ten days. Naturally, in such a short trip, we had no opportunity to see how things were with the country or the people.

'How are you going yourself, Jack?' I asked him.

'You seen this Walcott?' he says.

'Just in the gym.'

'Well,' Jack says, 'I'm going to need a lot of luck with that boy.'

'He can't hit you, Jack,' Soldier said.

'I wish to hell he couldn't.'

'He couldn't hit you with a handful of bird-shot.'

'Bird-shot'd be all right,' Jack says. 'I wouldn't mind bird-shot any.'

'He looks easy to hit,' I said.

'Sure,' Jack says, 'he ain't going to last long. He ain't going to last like you and me, Jerry. But right now he's got everything.'

'You'll left-hand him to death.'

'Maybe,' Jack says. 'Sure. I got a chance to.'

'Handle him like you handled Richie Lewis.'

'Richie Lewis,' Jack said. 'That kike!'

The three of us, Jack Brennan, Soldier Bartlett, and I, were in Handley's. There were a couple of broads sitting at the next table to us. They had been drinking.

'What do you mean, kike?' one of the broads says. 'What do you mean, kike, you big Irish bum?'

'Sure,' Jack says. 'That's it.'

'Kikes,' this broad goes on. 'They're always talking about kikes, these big Irishmen. What do you mean, kikes?'

'Come on. Let's get out of here.'

'Kikes,' this broad goes on. 'Whoever saw you ever buy a drink? Your wife sews your pockets up every morning. These Irishmen and their kikes! Richie Lewis could lick you too.'

'Sure,' Jack says. 'And you give away a lot of things free too, don't you?'

We went out. That was Jack. He could say what he wanted to when he wanted to say it.

Jack started training out at Danny Hogan's health farm over in Jersey. It was nice out there but Jack didn't like it much. He didn't like being away from his wife and the kids, and he was sore and grouchy most of the time. He liked me and we got along fine together; and he liked Hogan, but after a while Soldier Bartlett commenced to get on his nerves. A kidder gets to be an awful thing around a camp if his stuff goes sort of sour. Soldier was always kidding Jack, just sort of kidding him all the time. It wasn't very funny and it wasn't very good, and it began to get to Jack. It was sort of stuff like this. Jack would finish up with the weights and the bag and pull on the gloves.

'You want to work?' he'd say to Soldier.

'Sure. How you want me to work?' Soldier would ask. 'Want me to treat you rough like Walcott? Want me to knock you down a few times?'

'That's it,' Jack would say. He didn't like it any, though.

One morning we were all out on the road. We'd been out quite a way and now we were coming back. We'd go along fast for three minutes and then walk a minute, and then go fast for three minutes again. Jack wasn't ever what you would call a sprinter. He'd move around fast enough in the ring if he had to, but he wasn't any too fast on the road. All the time we were walking Soldier was kidding him. We came up the hill to the farmhouse.

'Well,' says Jack, 'you better go back to town, Soldier.'

'What do you mean?'

'You better go back to town and stay there.'

'What's the matter?'

'I'm sick of hearing you talk.'

'Yes?' says Soldier.

'Yes,' says Jack.

'You'll be a damn sight sicker when Walcott gets through with you.'

'Sure,' says Jack, 'maybe I will. But I know I'm sick of you.'

So Soldier went off on the train to town that same morning. I went with him to the train. He was good and sore.

'I was just kidding him,' he said. We were waiting on the platform. 'He can't pull that stuff with me, Jerry.'

'He's nervous and crabby,' I said. 'He's a good fellow, Soldier.'

'The hell he is. The hell he's ever been a good fellow.'

'Well,' I said, 'so long, Soldier.'

The train had come in. He climbed up with his bag.

'So long, Jerry,' he says. 'You be in town before the fight?'

'I don't think so.'

'See you then.'

He went in and the conductor swung up and the train went out. I rode back to the farm in the cart. Jack was on the porch writing a letter to his wife. The mail had come and I got the papers and went over on the other side of the porch and sat down to read. Hogan came out the door and walked over to me.

'Did he have a jam with Soldier?'

'Not a jam,' I said. 'He just told him to go back to town.'

'I could see it coming,' Hogan said. 'He never liked Soldier much.'

'No. He don't like many people.'

'He's a pretty cold one,' Hogan said.

'Well, he's always been fine to me.'

'Me too,' Hogan said. 'I got no kick on him. He's a cold one, though.'

Hogan went in through the screen door and I sat there on the porch and read the papers. It was just starting to get fall weather and it's nice country there in Jersey, up in the hills, and after I read the paper through I sat there and looked out at the country and the road down below against the woods with cars going along it, lifting the dust up. It was fine weather and pretty nice-looking country. Hogan came to the door and I said, 'Say, Hogan, haven't you got anything to shoot here?'

'No,' Hogan said. 'Only sparrows.'

'Seen the paper?' I said to Hogan.

'What's in it?'

'Sande booted three of them in yesterday.'

'I got that on the telephone last night.'

'You follow them pretty close, Hogan?' I asked.

'Oh, I keep in touch with them,' Hogan said.

'How about Jack?' I says. 'Does he still play them?'

'Him?' said Hogan. 'Can you see him doing it?'

Just then Jack came around the corner with the letter in his hand. He's wearing a sweater and an old pair of pants and boxing shoes.

'Got a stamp, Hogan?' he asks.

'Give me the letter,' Hogan said. 'I'll mail it for you.'

'Say Jack,' I said, 'didn't you used to play the ponies?'

'Sure.'

'I knew you did. I knew I used to see you out at Sheepshead.'

'What did you lay off them for?' Hogan asked.

'Lost money.'

Jack sat down on the porch by me. He leaned back against a post. He shut his eyes in the sun.

'Want a chair?' Hogan asked.

'No,' said Jack. 'This is fine.'

'It's a nice day,' I said. 'It's pretty nice out in the country.'

'I'd a damn sight rather be in town with the wife.'

'Well, you only got another week.'

'Yes,' Jack says. 'That's so.'

We sat there on the porch. Hogan was inside at the office.

'What do you think about the shape I'm in?' Jack asked me.

'Well, you can't tell,' I said. 'You got a week to get around into form.'

'Don't stall me.'

'Well,' I said, 'you're not right.'

'I'm not sleeping,' Jack said.

'You'll be all right in a couple of days.'

'No,' said Jack, 'I got the insomnia.'

'What's on your mind?'

'I miss the wife.'

'Have her come out.'

'No. I'm too old for that.'

'We'll take a long walk before you turn in and get you good and tired.'

'Tired!' Jack says. 'I'm tired all the time.'

He was that way all week. He wouldn't sleep at night and

he'd get up in the morning feeling that way, you know, when you can't shut your hands.

'He's stale as poorhouse cake,' Hogan said. 'He's nothing.'

'I never seen Walcott,' I said.

'He'll kill him,' said Hogan. 'He'll tear him in two.'

'Well,' I said, 'everybody's got to get it sometime.'

'Not like this, though,' Hogan said. 'They'll think he never trained. It gives the farm a black eye.'

'You hear what the reporters said about him?'

'Didn't I! They said he was awful. They said they oughtn't to let him fight.'

'Well,' I said, 'they're always wrong, ain't they?'

'Yes,' said Hogan. 'But this time they're right.'

'What the hell do they know about whether a man's right or not?'

'Well,' said Hogan, 'they're not such fools.'

'All they did was pick Willard at Toledo. This Lardner, he's so wise now, ask him about when he picked Willard at Toledo.'

'Aw, he wasn't out,' Hogan said. 'He only writes the big fights.'

'I don't care who they are,' I said. 'What the hell do they know? They can write maybe, but what the hell do they know?'

'You don't think Jack's in any shape, do you?' Hogan asked.

'No. He's through. All he needs is to have Corbett pick him to win for it to be all over.'

'Well, Corbett'll pick him,' Hogan says.

'Sure. He'll pick him.'

That night Jack didn't sleep any either. The next morning was the last day before the fight. After breakfast we were out on the porch again.

'What do you think about, Jack, when you can't sleep?' I said.

'Oh, I worry,' Jack says. 'I worry about property I got up in the Bronx, I worry about property I got in Florida. I worry about the kids. I worry about the wife. Sometimes I think about fights. I think about that kike Ted Lewis and I get sore.

73

I got some stocks and I worry about them. What the hell don't I think about?'

'Well,' I said, 'tomorrow night it'll all be over.'

'Sure,' said Jack. 'That always helps a lot, don't it? That just fixes everything all up, I suppose. Sure.'

He was sore all day. We didn't do any work. Jack just moved around a little to loosen up. He shadow-boxed a few rounds. He didn't even look good doing that. He skipped the rope a little while. He couldn't sweat.

'He'd be better not to do any work at all,' Hogan said. We were standing watching him skip rope. 'Don't he ever sweat at all any more?'

'He can't sweat.'

'Do you suppose he's got the con? He never had any trouble making weight, did he?'

'No, he hasn't got any con. He just hasn't got anything inside any more.'

'He ought to sweat,' said Hogan.

Jack came over, skipping the rope. He was skipping up and down in front of us, forward and back, crossing his arms every third time.

'Well,' he says. 'What are you buzzards talking about?'

'I don't think you ought to work any more,' Hogan says. 'You'll be stale.'

'Wouldn't that be awful?' Jack says and skips away down the floor, slapping the rope hard.

That afternoon John Collins showed up out at the farm. Jack was up in his room. John came out in a car from town. He had a couple of friends with him. The car stopped and they all got out.

'Where's Jack?' John asked me.

'Up in his room, lying down.'

'Lying down?'

'Yes,' I said.

'How is he?'

I looked at the two fellows that were with John.

'They're friends of his,' John said.

'He's pretty bad,' I said.

'What's the matter with him?'

'He don't sleep.'

'Hell,' said John. 'That Irishman could never sleep.'

'He isn't right,' I said.

'Hell,' John said. 'He's never right. I've had him for ten years and he's never been right yet.'

The fellows who were with him laughed.

'I want you to shake hands with Mr Morgan and Mr Steinfelt,' John said. 'This is Mr Doyle. He's been training Jack.'

'Glad to meet you,' I said.

'Let's go up and see the boy,' the fellow called Morgan said.

'Let's have a look at him,' Steinfelt said.

We all went upstairs.

'Where's Hogan?' John asked.

'He's out in the barn with a couple of his customers,' I said.

'He got many people out here now?' John asked.

'Just two.'

'Pretty quiet, ain't it?' Morgan said.

'Yes,' I said. 'It's pretty quiet.'

We were outside Jack's room. John knocked on the door. There wasn't any answer.

'Maybe he's asleep,' I said.

'What the hell's he sleeping in the daytime for?'

John turned the handle and we all went in. Jack was lying asleep on the bed. He was face down and his face was in the pillow. Both his arms were around the pillow.

'Hey, Jack!' John said to him.

Jack's head moved a little on the pillow. 'Jack!' John says, leaning over him. Jack just dug a little deeper in the pillow. John touched him on the shoulder. Jack sat up and looked at us. He hadn't shaved and he was wearing an old sweater.

'Christ! Why can't you let me sleep?' he says to John.

'Don't be sore,' John says. 'I didn't mean to wake you up.'

'Oh no,' Jack says. 'Of course not.'

'You know Morgan and Steinfelt,' John said.

'Glad to see you,' Jack says.

'How do you feel, Jack?' Morgan asks him.

'Fine,' Jack says. 'How the hell would I feel?'

'You look fine,' Steinfelt says.

'Yes, don't I,' says Jack. 'Say,' he says to John. 'You're my manager. You get a big enough cut. Why the hell don't you come out here when the reporters was out! You want Jerry and me to talk to them?'

'I had Lew fighting in Philadelphia,' John said.

'What the hell's that to me?' Jack says. 'You're my manager. You get a big enough cut, don't you? You aren't making me any money in Philadelphia, are you? Why the hell aren't you out here when I ought to have you?'

'Hogan was here.'

'Hogan,' Jack says. 'Hogan's as dumb as I am.'

'Soldier Bartlett was out here wukking with you for a while, wasn't he?' Steinfelt said to change the subject.

'Yes, he was out here,' Jack says. 'He was out here all right.'

'Say, Jerry,' John said to me. 'Would you go and find Hogan and tell him we want to see him in about half-an-hour?'

'Sure,' I said.

'Why the hell can't he stick around?' Jack says. 'Stick around, Jerry.'

Morgan and Steinfelt looked at each other.

'Quiet down, Jack,' John said to him.

'I better go find Hogan,' I said.

'All right, if you want to go,' Jack says. 'None of these guys are going to send you away, though.'

'I'll go find Hogan,' I said.

Hogan was out in the gym in the barn. He had a couple of his health-farm patients with the gloves on. They neither one wanted to hit the other, for fear the other would come back and hit him.

'That'll do,' Hogan said when he saw me come in. 'You can stop the slaughter. You gentlemen take a shower and Bruce will rub you down.'

They climbed out through the ropes and Hogan came over to me.

'John Collins is out with a couple of friends to see Jack,' I said.

'I saw them come up in the car.'

'Who are the two fellows with John?'

76

'They're what you call wise boys,' Hogan said. 'Don't you know them two?'

'No,' I said.

'That's Happy Steinfelt and Lew Morgan. They got a pool-room.'

'I been away a long time,' I said.

'Sure,' said Hogan. 'That Happy Steinfelt's a big operator.'

'I've heard his name,' I said.

'He's a pretty smooth boy,' Hogan said. 'They're a couple of sharpshooters.'

'Well,' I said. 'They want to see us in half-an-hour.'

'You mean they don't want to see us until half-an-hour?'

'That's it.'

'Come on in the office,' Hogan said. 'To hell with those sharpshooters.'

After about thirty minutes or so Hogan and I went up-stairs. We knocked on Jack's door. They were talking inside the room.

'Wait a minute,' somebody said.

'To hell with that stuff,' Hogan said. 'When you want to see me I'm down in the office.'

We heard the door unlock. Steinfelt opened it.

'Come on in, Hogan,' he says. 'We're all going to have a drink.'

'Well,' says Hogan. 'That's something.'

We went in. Jack was sitting on the bed. John and Morgan were sitting on a couple of chairs. Steinfelt was standing up.

'You're a pretty mysterious lot of boys,' Hogan said.

'Hello, Danny,' John says.

'Hello, Danny,' Morgan says and shakes hands.

Jack doesn't say anything. He just sits there on the bed. He ain't with the others. He's all by himself. He was wearing an old blue jersey and pants and had on boxing shoes. He needed a shave. Steinfelt and Morgan were dressers. John was quite a dresser too. Jack sat there looking Irish and tough.

Steinfelt brought out a bottle and Hogan brought in some glasses and everybody had a drink. Jack and I took one and the rest of them went on and had two or three each.

'Better save some for your ride back,' Hogan said.

77

'Don't you worry. We got plenty,' Morgan said.

Jack hadn't drunk anything since the one drink. He was standing up and looking at them. Morgan was sitting on the bed where Jack had sat.

'Have a drink, Jack,' John said and handed him the glass and the bottle.

'No,' Jack said, 'I never liked to go to these wakes.'

They all laughed. Jack didn't laugh.

They were all feeling pretty good when they left. Jack stood on the porch when they got into the car. They waved to him.

'So long,' Jack said.

We had supper. Jack didn't say anything all during the meal except, 'Will you pass me this?' or 'Will you pass me that?' The two health-farm patients ate at the same table with us. They were pretty nice fellows. After we finished eating we went out on the porch. It was dark early.

'Like to take a walk, Jerry?' Jack asked.

'Sure,' I said.

We put on our coats and started out. It was quite a way down to the main road and then we walked along the main road about a mile and a half. Cars kept going by and we would pull out to the side until they were past. Jack didn't say anything. After we had stepped out into the bushes to let a big car go by Jack said, 'To hell with this walking. Come on back to Hogan's.'

We went along a side road that cut up over the hill and cut across the fields back to Hogan's. We could see the lights of the house up on the hill. We came around to the front of the house and there standing in the doorway was Hogan.

'Have a good walk?' Hogan asked.

'Oh, fine,' Jack said. 'Listen, Hogan. Have you got any liquor?'

'Sure,' says Hogan. 'What's the idea?'

'Send it up to the room,' Jack says. 'I'm going to sleep tonight.'

'You're the doctor,' Hogan says.

'Come on up to the room, Jerry,' Jack says.

Upstairs, Jack sat on the bed with his head in his hands.

'Ain't it a life?' Jack says.

Hogan brought in a quart of liquor and two glasses.

'Want some ginger ale?'

'What do you think I want to do, get sick?'

'I just asked you,' said Hogan.

'Have a drink?' said Jack.

'No, thanks,' said Hogan. He went out.

'How about it, Jerry?'

'I'll have one with you,' I said.

Jack poured out a couple of drinks. 'Now,' he said, 'I want to take it slow and easy.'

'Put some water in it,' I said.

'Yes,' Jack said. 'I guess that's better.'

We had a couple of drinks without saying anything. Jack started to pour me another.

'No,' I said, 'that's all I want.'

'All right,' Jack said. He poured himself out another big shot and put water in it. He was lighting up a little.

'That was a fine bunch out here this afternoon,' he said. 'They don't take any chances, those two.'

Then a little later, 'Well,' he says, 'they're right. What the hell's the good in taking chances?'

'Don't you want another, Jerry?' he said. 'Come on, drink along with me.'

'I don't need it, Jack,' I said. 'I feel all right.'

'Just have one more,' Jack said. It was softening him up.

'All right,' I said.

Jack poured one for me and another big one for himself.

'You know,' he said, 'I like liquor pretty well. If I hadn't been boxing I would have drunk quite a lot.'

'Sure,' I said.

'You know,' he said, 'I missed a lot, boxing.'

'You made plenty of money.'

'Sure, that's what I'm after. You know I miss a lot, Jerry.'

'How do you mean?'

'Well,' he says, 'like about the wife. And being away from home so much. It don't do my girls any good. "Who's your old man?" some of those society kids'll say to them. "My old man's Jack Brennan." That don't do them any good.'

'Hell,' I said, 'all that makes a difference is if they got dough.'

'Well,' says Jack, 'I got the dough for them all right.'

He poured out another drink. The bottle was about empty.

'Put some water in it,' I said. Jack poured in some water.

'You know,' he says, 'you ain't got any idea how I miss the wife.'

'Sure.'

'You ain't got any idea. You can't have an idea what it's like.'

'It ought to be better out in the country than in town.'

'With me now,' Jack said, 'it don't make any difference where I am. You can't have an idea what it's like.'

'Have another drink.'

'Am I getting soused? Do I talk funny?'

'You're coming on all right.'

'You can't have an idea what it's like. They ain't anybody can have an idea what it's like.'

'Except the wife,' I said.

'She knows,' Jack said. 'She knows all right. She knows. You bet she knows.'

'Put some water in that,' I said.

'Jerry,' says Jack, 'you can't have an idea what it gets to be like.'

He was good and drunk. He was looking at me steady. His eyes were sort of too steady.

'You'll sleep all right,' I said.

'Listen, Jerry,' Jack says. 'You want to make some money? Get some money down on Walcott.'

'Yes?'

'Listen, Jerry.' Jack put down the glass. 'I'm not drunk now, see? You know what I'm betting on him? Fifty grand.'

'That's a lot of dough.'

'Fifty grand,' Jack says, 'at two to one. I'll get twenty-five thousand bucks. Get some money on him, Jerry.'

'It sounds good,' I said.

'How can I beat him?' Jack says. 'It ain't crooked. How can I beat him? Why not make money on it?'

'Put some water in that,' I said.

'I'm through after this fight,' Jack says. 'I'm through with it. I got to take a beating. Why shouldn't I make money on it?'

'Sure.'

'I ain't slept for a week,' Jack says. 'All night I lay awake and worry my can off. I can't sleep, Jerry. You ain't got an idea what it's like when you can't sleep.'

'Sure.'

'I can't sleep. That's all. I just can't sleep. What's the use of taking care of yourself all these years when you can't sleep?'

'It's bad.'

'You ain't got an idea what it's like, Jerry, when you can't sleep.'

'Put some water in that,' I said.

Well, about eleven o'clock Jack passes out and I put him to bed. Finally he's so he can't keep from sleeping. I helped him get his clothes off and got him into bed.

'You'll sleep all right, Jack,' I said.

'Sure,' Jack says, 'I'll sleep now.'

'Goodnight, Jack,' I said.

'Goodnight, Jerry,' Jack says. 'You're the only friend I got.'

'Oh, hell,' I said.

'You're the only friend I got,' Jack says, 'the only friend I got.'

'Go to sleep,' I said.

'I'll sleep,' Jack says.

Downstairs, Hogan was sitting at the desk in the office reading the papers. He looked up. 'Well, you get your boy friend to sleep?' he asks.

'He's off.'

'It's better for him than not sleeping,' Hogan said.

'Sure.'

'You'd have a hell of a time explaining that to these sports writers though,' Hogan said.

'Well, I'm going to bed myself,' I said.

'Goodnight,' said Hogan.

In the morning I came downstairs about eight o'clock and got some breakfast. Hogan had his customers out in the barn doing exercises. I went out and watched them.

'One! Two! Three! Four!' Hogan was counting for them. 'Hello, Jerry,' he said. 'Is Jack up yet?'

'No. He's still sleeping.'

I went back to my room and packed up to go in to town. About nine-thirty I heard Jack getting up in the next room. When I heard him go downstairs I went down after him. Jack was sitting at the breakfast table. Hogan had come in and was standing beside the table.

'How do you feel, Jack?' I asked him.

'Not so bad.'

'Sleep well?' Hogan asked.

'I slept all right,' Jack said. 'I got a thick tongue but I ain't got a head.'

'Good,' said Hogan. 'That was good liquor.'

'Put it on the bill,' Jack says.

'What time you want to go into town?' Hogan asked.

'Before lunch,' Jack says. 'The eleven o'clock train.'

'Sit down, Jerry,' Jack said. Hogan went out.

I sat down at the table. Jack was eating a grapefruit. When he'd find a seed he'd spit it out in the spoon and dump it on the plate.

'I guess I was pretty stewed last night,' he started.

'You drank some liquor.'

'I guess I said a lot of fool things.'

'You weren't bad.'

'Where's Hogan?' he asked. He was through with the grapefruit.

'He's out in front in the office.'

'What did I say about betting on the fight?' Jack asked. He was holding the spoon and sort of poking at the grapefruit with it.

The girl came in with some ham and eggs and took away the grapefruit.

'Bring me another glass of milk,' Jack said to her. She went out.

'You said you had fifty grand on Walcott,' I said.

'That's right,' Jack said.

'That's a lot of money.'

'I don't feel too good about it,' Jack said.

82

'Something might happen.'

'No,' Jack said. 'He wants the title bad. They'll be shooting with him all right.'

'You can't ever tell.'

'No. He wants the title. It's worth a lot of money to him.'

'Fifty grand is a lot of money,' I said.

'It's business,' said Jack. 'I can't win. You know I can't win anyway.'

'As long as you're in there you got a chance.'

'No,' Jack says. 'I'm all through. It's just business.'

'How do you feel?'

'Pretty good,' Jack said. 'The sleep was what I needed.'

'You might go good.'

'I'll give them a good show,' Jack said.

After breakfast Jack called up his wife on the long-distance. He was inside the booth telephoning.

'That's the first time he's called her up since he's out here,' Hogan said.

'He writes her every day.'

'Sure,' Hogan says, 'a letter only costs two cents.'

Hogan said goodbye to us and Bruce, the nigger rubber, drove us down to the train in the cart.

'Goodbye, Mr Brennan,' Bruce said at the train, 'I sure hope you knock his can off.'

'So long,' Jack said. He gave Bruce two dollars. Bruce had worked on him a lot. He looked kind of disappointed. Jack saw me looking at Bruce holding the two dollars.

'It's all in the bill,' he said. 'Hogan charged me for the rubbing.'

On the train going to town Jack didn't talk. He sat in the corner of the seat with his ticket in his hat-band and looked out of the window. Once he turned and spoke to me.

'I told the wife I'd take a room at the Shelby tonight,' he said. 'It's just around the corner from the Garden. I can go up to the house tomorrow morning.'

'That's a good idea,' I said. 'Your wife ever see you fight, Jack?'

'No,' Jack says. 'She never seen me fight.'

I thought he must be figuring on taking an awful beating if

he doesn't want to go home afterwards. In town we took a taxi up to the Shelby. A boy came out and took our bags and we went to the desk.

'How much are the rooms?' Jack asked.

'We only have double rooms,' the clerk says. 'I can give you a nice double room for ten dollars.'

'That's too steep.'

'I can give you a double room for seven dollars.'

'With a bath?'

'Certainly.'

'You might as well bunk with me, Jerry,' Jack says.

'Oh,' I said, 'I'll sleep down at my brother-in-law's.'

'I don't mean for you to pay it,' Jack says. 'I just want to get my money's worth.'

'Will you register, please?' the clerk says. He looked at the names. 'Number 238, Mister Brennan.'

We went up in the elevator. It was a nice big room with two beds and a door opening into a bathroom.

'This is pretty good,' Jack says.

The boy who brought us up pulled up the curtains and brought in our bags. Jack didn't make any move, so I gave the boy a quarter. We washed up and Jack said we better go out and get something to eat.

We ate lunch at Jimmey Handley's place. Quite a lot of the boys were there. When we were about half through eating, John came in and sat down with us. Jack didn't talk much.

'How are you on the weight, Jack?' John asked him. Jack was putting away a pretty good lunch.

'I could make it with my clothes on,' Jack said. He never had to worry about taking off weight. He was a natural welter-weight and he'd never gotten fat. He'd lost weight out at Hogan's.

'Well, that's one thing you never had to worry about,' John said.

'That's one thing,' Jack says.

We went around to the Garden to weigh in after lunch. The match was made at a hundred forty-seven pounds at three o'clock. Jack stepped on the scales with a towel around him.

The bar didn't move. Walcott had just weighed and was standing with a lot of people around him.

'Let's see what you weigh, Jack,' Freedman, Walcott's manager said.

'All right, weigh *him* then,' Jack jerked his head towards Walcott.

'Drop the towel,' Freedman said.

'What do you make it?' Jack asked the fellows who were weighing.

'One hundred and forty-three pounds,' the fat man who was weighing said.

'You're down fine, Jack,' Freedman says.

'Weigh *him*,' Jack says.

Walcott came over. He was a blond with wide shoulders and arms like a heavy-weight. He didn't have much legs. Jack stood about half-a-head taller than he did.

'Hello, Jack,' he said. His face was plenty marked up.

'Hello,' said Jack. 'How you feel?'

'Good,' Walcott says. He dropped the towel from around his waist and stood on the scales. He had the widest shoulders and back you ever saw.

'One hundred and forty-six pounds and twelve ounces.'

Walcott stepped off and grinned at Jack.

'Well,' John says to him, 'Jack's spotting you about four pounds.'

'More than that when I come in, kid,' Walcott says. 'I'm going to go and eat now.'

We went back and Jack got dressed. 'He's a pretty tough-looking boy,' Jack says to me.

'He looks as though he's been hit plenty of times.'

'Oh, yes,' Jack says. 'He ain't hard to hit.'

'Where are you going?' John asked when Jack was dressed.

'Back to the hotel,' Jack says. 'You looked after everything?'

'Yes,' John says. 'It's all looked after.'

'I'm going to lie down for awhile,' Jack says.

'I'll come around for you about a quarter to seven and we'll go and eat.'

'All right.'

Up at the hotel Jack took off his shoes and his coat and lay down for awhile. I wrote a letter. I looked over a couple of times and Jack wasn't sleeping. He was lying perfectly still but every once in a while his eyes would open. Finally he sits up.

'Want to play some cribbage, Jerry?' he says.

'Sure,' I said.

He went over to his suitcase and got out the cards and the cribbage board. We played cribbage and he won three dollars off me. John knocked at the door and came in.

'Want to play some cribbage, John?' Jack asked him.

John put his kelly down on the table. It was all wet. His coat was wet too.

'Is it raining?' Jack asks.

'It's pouring,' John says. 'The taxi I had, got tied up in the traffic and I got out and walked.'

'Come on, play some cribbage,' Jack says.

'You ought to go and eat.'

'No,' says Jack. 'I don't want to eat yet.'

So they played cribbage for about half-an-hour and Jack won a dollar and a half off him.

'Well, I suppose we got to go eat,' Jack says. He went to the window and looked out.

'Is it still raining?'

'Yes.'

'Let's eat in the hotel,' John says.

'All right,' Jack says, 'I'll play you once more to see who pays for the meal.'

After a little while Jack gets up and says, 'You buy the meal, John,' and we went downstairs and ate in the big dining-room.

After we ate we went upstairs and Jack played cribbage with John again and won two dollars and a half off him. Jack was feeling pretty good. John had a bag with him with all his stuff in it. Jack took off his shirt and collar and put on a jersey and a sweater, so he wouldn't catch cold when he came out, and put his ring clothes and bathrobe in a bag.

'You all ready?' John asks him. 'I'll call up and have them get a taxi.'

Pretty soon the telephone rang and they said the taxi was waiting.

We rode down in the elevator and went out through the lobby, and got in a taxi and rode around to the Garden. It was raining hard but there was a lot of people outside on the streets. The Garden was sold out. As we came in on our way to the dressing-room I saw how full it was. It looked like half-a-mile down to the ring. It was all dark. Just the lights over the ring.

'It's a good thing, with this rain, they didn't try to pull this fight in the ball park,' John said.

'They got a good crowd,' Jack says.

'This is a fight that would draw a lot more than the Garden could hold.'

'You can't tell about the weather,' Jack says.

John came to the door of the dressing-room and poked his head in. Jack was sitting there with his bathrobe on, he had his arms folded and was looking at the floor. John had a couple of handlers with him. They looked over his shoulder. Jack looked up.

'Is he in?' he asked.

'He's just gone down,' John said.

We started down. Walcott was just getting into the ring. The crowd gave him a big hand. He climbed through between the ropes and put his two fists together and smiled, and shook them at the crowd, first at one side of the ring, then at the other, and then sat down. Jack got a good hand coming down through the crowd. Jack is Irish and the Irish always get a pretty good hand. An Irishman don't draw in New York like a Jew or an Italian, but they always get a good hand. Jack climbed up and bent down to go through the ropes and Walcott came over from his corner and pushed the rope down for Jack to go through. The crowd thought that was wonderful. Walcott put his hand on Jack's shoulder and they stood there just for a second.

'So you're going to be one of these popular champions,' Jack says to him. 'Take your goddam hand off my shoulder.'

'Be yourself,' Walcott says.

This is all great for the crowd. How gentlemanly the boys

are before the fight! How they wish each other luck!

Solly Freedman came over to our corner while Jack is bandaging his hands and John is over in Walcott's corner. Jack puts his thumb through the slit in the bandage and then wrapped his hand nice and smooth. I taped it around the wrist and twice across the knuckles.

'Hey,' Freedman says. 'Where do you get all that tape?'

'Feel of it,' Jack says. 'It's soft, ain't it? Don't be a hick.'

Freedman stands there all the time while Jack bandages the other hand, and one of the boys that's going to handle him brings the gloves and I pull them on and work them around.

'Say, Freedman,' Jack asks, 'what nationality is this Walcott?'

'I don't know,' Solly says. 'He's some sort of a Dane.'

'He's a Bohemian,' the lad who brought the gloves said.

The referee called them out to the centre of the ring and Jack walks out. Walcott comes out smiling. They met and the referee put his arm on each of their shoulders.

'Hello, popularity,' Jack says to Walcott.

'Be yourself.'

'What do you call yourself "Walcott" for?' Jacks says. 'Didn't you know he was a nigger?'

'Listen –' says the referee, and he gives them the same old line. Once Walcott interrupts him. He grabs Jack's arm and says, 'Can I hit when he's got me like this?'

'Keep your hands off me,' Jack says. 'There ain't no moving-pictures of this.'

They went back to their corners. I lifted the bathrobe off Jack and he leaned on the ropes and flexed his knees a couple of times and scuffed his shoes in the rosin. The gong rang and Jack turned quick and went out. Walcott came towards him and they touched gloves and as soon as Walcott dropped his hands Jack jumped his left into his face twice. There wasn't anybody ever boxed better than Jack. Walcott was after him, going forward all the time with his chin on his chest. He's a hooker and he carries his hands pretty low. All he knows is to get in there and sock. But every time he gets in there close, Jack has the left hand in his face. It's just as though it's automatic. Jack just raises the left hand up and it's in Walcott's face. Three or four times Jack brings the right over but Walcott gets it on the shoulder or high up on the head. He's just like all these hookers. The only thing he's afraid of is another one of the same kind. He's covered everywhere you can hurt him. He don't care about a left hand in his face.

After about four rounds Jack has him bleeding bad and his face all cut up, but every time Walcott's got in close he's socked so hard he's got two big red patches on both sides just below Jack's ribs. Every time he gets in close, Jack ties him up, then gets one hand loose and uppercuts him, but when Walcott gets his hands loose he socks Jack in the body so they can hear it outside in the street. He's a socker.

It goes along like that for three rounds more. They don't talk any. They're working all the time. We worked over Jack plenty too, in between the rounds. He don't look good at all but he never does much work in the ring. He don't move around much and that left hand is just automatic. It's just like it was connected with Walcott's face and Jack just had to wish it in every time. Jack is always calm in close and he doesn't waste any juice. He knows everything about working in close too and he's getting away with a lot of stuff. While they were in our corner I watched him tie Walcott up, get his right hand loose, turn it and come up with an uppercut that got Walcott's nose with the heel of the glove. Walcott was bleeding bad and leaned his nose on Jack's shoulder so as to give Jack some of it too, and Jack sort of lifted his shoulder sharp and caught him against the nose, and then brought down the right hand and did the same thing again.

Walcott was sore as hell. By the time they'd gone five rounds he hated Jack's guts. Jack wasn't sore; that is, he wasn't any sorer than he always was. He certainly did used to make the fellows he fought hate boxing. That was why he hated Kid Lewis so. He never got Kid's goat. Kid Lewis always had about three new dirty things Jack couldn't do. Jack was as safe as a church all the time he was in there, as long as he was strong. He certainly was treating Walcott rough. The funny thing was it looked as though Jack was an open classic boxer. That was because he had all that stuff too.

After the seventh round Jack says, 'My left's getting heavy.'
From then he started to take a beating. It didn't show at

89

first. But instead of him running the fight it was Walcott was running it, instead of being safe all the time now he was in trouble. He couldn't keep him out with the left hand now. It looked as though it was the same as ever, only now instead of Walcott's punches just missing him they were just hitting him. He took an awful beating in the body.

'What's the round?' Jack asked.

'The eleventh.'

'I can't stay,' Jack says. 'My legs are going bad.'

Walcott had been just hitting him for a long time. It was like a baseball catcher pulls the ball and takes some of the shock off. From now on Walcott commenced to land solid. He certainly was a socking-machine. Jack was just trying to block everything now. It didn't show what an awful beating he was taking. In between the rounds I worked on his legs. The muscles would flutter under my hands all the time I was rubbing them. He was sick as hell.

'How's it go?' he asked John, turning around, his face all swollen.

'It's his fight.'

'I think I can last,' Jack says. 'I don't want this bohunk to stop me.'

It was going just the way he thought it would. He knew he couldn't beat Walcott. He wasn't strong any more. He was all right though. His money was all right and now he wanted to finish it off right to please himself. He didn't want to be knocked out.

The gong rang and we pushed him out. He went out slow. Walcott came right out after him. Jack put the left in his face and Walcott took it, came in under it and started working on Jack's body. Jack tried to tie him up and it was just like trying to hold on to a buzz-saw. Jack broke away from it and missed with the right. Walcott clipped him with a left hook and Jack went down. He went down on his hands and knees and looked at us. The referee started counting. Jack was watching us and shaking his head. At eight John motioned to him. You couldn't hear on account of the crowd. Jack got up. The referee had been holding Walcott back with one arm while he counted.

When Jack was on his feet Walcott started towards him.

'Watch yourself, Jimmy,' I heard Solly Freedman yell to him.

Walcott came up to Jack looking at him. Jack stuck the left hand at him. Walcott just shook his head. He backed Jack up against the ropes, measured him and then hooked the left very light to the side of Jack's head and socked the right into the body as hard as he could sock, just as low as he could get it. He must have hit him five inches below the belt. I thought the eyes would come out of Jack's head. They stuck way out. His mouth came open.

The referee grabbed Walcott. Jack stepped forward. If he went down there went fifty thousand bucks. He walked as though all his insides were going to fall out.

'It wasn't low,' he said. 'It was an accident.'

The crowd were yelling so you couldn't hear anything.

'I'm all right,' Jack says. They were right in front of us. The referee looks at John and then he shakes his head.

'Come on, you polak son-of-a-bitch,' Jack says to Walcott.

John was hanging on to the ropes. He had the towel ready to chuck in. Jack was standing just a little way out from the ropes. He took a step forward. I saw the sweat come out on his face like somebody had squeezed it and a big drop went down his nose.

'Come on and fight,' Jack says to Walcott.

The referee looked at John and waved Walcott on.

'Go in there, you slob,' he says.

Walcott went in. He didn't know what to do either. He never thought Jack could have stood it. Jack put the left in his face. There was such a hell of a lot of yelling going on. They were right in front of us. Walcott hit him twice. Jack's face was the worst thing I ever saw, – the look on it! He was holding himself and all his body together and it all showed on his face. All the time he was thinking and holding his body in where it was busted.

Then he started to sock. His face looked awful all the time. He started to sock with his hands low down by his side, swinging at Walcott. Walcott covered up and Jack was swinging wild at Walcott's head. Then he swung the left and it hit

Walcott in the groin and the right hit Walcott right bang where he'd hit Jack. Way low below the belt. Walcott went down and grabbed himself there and rolled and twisted around.

The referee grabbed Jack and pushed him towards his corner. John jumps into the ring. There was all this yelling going on. The referee was talking with the judges and then the announcer got into the ring with the megaphone and says, 'Walcott on a foul.'

The referee is talking to John and he says, 'What could I do? Jack wouldn't take the foul. Then when he's groggy he fouls him.'

'He'd lost it anyway,' John says.

Jack's sitting on the chair. I've got his gloves off and he's holding himself in down there with both hands. When he's got something supporting it his face doesn't look so bad.

'Go over and say you're sorry,' John says into his ear. 'It'll look good.'

Jack stands up and the sweat comes out all over his face. I put the bathrobe around him and he holds himself in with one hand under the bathrobe and goes across the ring. They've picked Walcott up and they're working on him. There're a lot of people in Walcott's corner. Nobody speaks to Jack. He leans over Walcott.

'I'm sorry,' Jack says. 'I didn't mean to foul you.'

Walcott doesn't say anything. He looks too damned sick.

'Well, you're the champion now,' Jack says to him. 'I hope you get a hell of a lot of fun out of it.'

'Leave the kid alone,' Solly Freedman says.

'Hello, Solly,' Jack says. 'I'm sorry I fouled your boy.'

Freedman just looks at him.

Jack went to his corner walking that funny jerky way and we got him down through the ropes and through the reporters' tables and out down the aisle. A lot of people want to slap Jack on the back. He goes out through all that mob in his bathrobe to the dressing-room. It's a popular win for Walcott. That's the way the money was bet in the Garden.

Once we got inside the dressing-room, Jack lay down and shut his eyes.

'We want to get to the hotel and get a doctor,' John says.

'I'm all busted inside,' Jack says.

'I'm sorry as hell, Jack,' John says.

'It's all right,' Jack says.

He lies there with his eyes shut.

'They certainly tried a nice double-cross,' John said.

'Your friends Morgan and Steinfelt,' Jack said. 'You got nice friends.'

He lies there, his eyes are open now. His face has still got that awful drawn look.

'It's funny how fast you can think when it means that much money,' Jack says.

'You're some boy, Jack,' John says.

'No,' Jack says. 'It was nothing.'

A SIMPLE ENQUIRY

Outside, the snow was higher than the window. The sunlight came in through the window and shone on a map on the pine-board wall of the hut. The sun was high and the light came in over the top of the snow. A trench had been cut along the open side of the hut, and each clear day the sun, shining on the wall, reflected heat against the snow and widened the trench. It was late March. The major sat at a table against the wall. His adjutant sat at another table.

Around the major's eyes were two white circles where his snow-glasses had protected his face from the sun on the snow. The rest of his face had been burned and then tanned and then burned through the tan. His nose was swollen and there were edges of loose skin where blisters had been. While he worked at the papers he put the fingers of his left hand into a saucer of oil and then spread the oil over his face, touching it very gently with the tips of his fingers. He was very careful to drain his fingers on the edge of the saucer so there was only a film of oil on them, and after he had stroked his forehead and his cheeks, he stroked his nose very delicately between his fingers. When he had finished he stood up, took the saucer of oil and went into the small room of the hut where he slept. 'I'm going to take a little sleep,' he said to the adjutant. In that army an adjutant is not a commissioned officer. 'You'll finish up.'

'Yes, signor maggiore,' the adjutant answered. He leaned back in his chair and yawned. He took a paper-covered book out of the pocket of his coat and opened it; then laid it down on the table and lit his pipe. He leaned forward on the table to read and puffed at his pipe. Then he closed the book and put it back in his pocket. He had too much paper-work to get through. He could not enjoy reading until it was done. Outside, the sun went behind a mountain and there was no more light on the wall of the hut. A soldier came in and put some pine branches, chopped into irregular lengths, into the stove. 'Be soft, Pinin,' the adjutant said to him. 'The major is sleeping.'

Pinin was the major's orderly. He was a dark-faced boy, and he fixed the stove, putting the pine wood in carefully, shut the door, and went into the back of the hut again. The adjutant went on with his papers.

'Tonani,' the major called.

'Signor maggiore?'

'Send Pinin in to me.'

'Pinin!' the adjutant called. Pinin came into the room. 'The major wants you,' the adjutant said.

Pinin walked across the main room of the hut towards the major's door. He knocked on the half-opened door. 'Signor maggiore?'

'Come in,' the adjutant heard the major say, 'and shut the door.'

Inside the room the major lay on his bunk. Pinin stood beside the bunk. The major lay with his head on the rucksack that he had stuffed with spare clothing to make a pillow. His long, burned, oiled face looked at Pinin. His hands lay on the blankets.

'You are nineteen?' he asked.

'Yes, signor maggiore.'

'You have ever been in love?'

'How do you mean, signor maggiore?'

'In love – with a girl?'

'I have been with girls.'

'I did not ask that. I asked if you had been in love – with a girl.'

'Yes, signor maggiore.'

'You are in love with this girl now? You don't write her. I read all your letters.'

'I am in love with her,' Pinin said, 'but I do not write her.'

'You are sure of this?'

'I am sure.'

'Tonani,' the major said in the same tone of voice, 'can you hear me talking?'

There was no answer from the next room.

'He cannot hear,' the major said. 'And you are quite sure that you love a girl?'

'I am sure.'

95

'And,' the major looked at him quickly, 'that you are not corrupt?'

'I don't know what you mean, corrupt.'

'All right,' the major said. 'You needn't be superior.'

Pinin looked at the floor. The major looked at his brown face, down and up him, and at his hands. Then he went on, not smiling. 'And you don't really want –' the major paused. Pinin looked at the floor. 'That your great desire isn't really –' Pinin looked at the floor. The major leaned his head back on the rucksack and smiled. He was really relieved: life in the army was too complicated. 'You're a good boy,' he said. 'You're a good boy, Pinin. But don't be superior and be careful someone else doesn't come along and take you.'

Pinin stood still beside the bunk.

'Don't be afraid,' the major said. His hands were folded on the blankets. 'I won't touch you. You can go back to your platoon if you like. But you had better stay on as my servant. You've less chance of being killed.'

'Do you want anything of me, signor maggiore?'

'No,' the major said. 'Go on and get on with whatever you were doing. Leave the door open when you go out.'

Pinin went out, leaving the door open. The adjutant looked up at him as he walked awkwardly across the room and out of the door. Pinin was flushed and moved differently than he had moved when he brought in the wood for the fire. The adjutant looked after him and smiled. Pinin came in with more wood for the stove. The major, lying on his bunk, looking at his cloth-covered helmet and his snow-glasses that hung from a nail on the wall, heard him walk across the floor. The little devil, he thought, I wonder if he lied to me.

After one Fourth of July, Nick, driving home late from town in the big waggon with Joe Garner and his family, passed nine drunken Indians along the road. He remembered there were nine because Joe Garner, driving along in the dusk, pulled up the horses, jumped down into the road and dragged an Indian out of the wheel rut. The Indian had been asleep, face down in the sand. Joe dragged him into the bushes and got back up on the waggon-box.

'That makes nine of them,' Joe said, 'just between here and the edge of town.'

'Them Indians,' said Mrs Garner.

Nick was on the back seat with the two Garner boys. He was looking out from the back seat to see the Indian where Joe had dragged him alongside of the road.

'Was it Billy Tabeshaw?' Carl asked.

'No.'

'His pants looked mighty like Billy.'

'All Indians wear the same kind of pants.'

'I didn't see him at all,' Frank said. 'Pa was down into the road and back up again before I seen a thing. I thought he was killing a snake.'

'Plenty of Indians'll kill snakes tonight, I guess,' Joe Garner said.

'Them Indians,' said Mrs Garner.

They drove along. The road turned off from the main highway and went up into the hills. It was hard pulling for the horses and the boys got down and walked. The road was sandy. Nick looked back from the top of the hill by the schoolhouse. He saw the lights of Petoskey and, off across Little Traverse Bay, the lights of Harbor Springs. They climbed back in the waggon again.

'They ought to put some gravel on that stretch,' Joe Garner said. The waggon went along the road through the woods. Joe and Mrs Garner sat close together on the front seat. Nick sat between the two boys. The road came out into a clearing.

'Right here was where Pa ran over the skunk.'

'It was further on.'

'It don't make no difference where it was,' Joe said without turning his head. 'One place is just as good as another to run over a skunk.'

'I saw two skunks last night,' Nick said.

'Where?'

'Down by the lake. They were looking for dead fish along the beach.'

'They were coons probably,' Carl said.

'They were skunks. I guess I know skunks.'

'You ought to,' Carl said. 'You got an Indian girl.'

'Stop talking that way, Carl,' said Mrs Garner.

'Well, they smell about the same.'

Joe Garner laughed.

'You stop laughing, Joe,' Mrs Garner said. 'I won't have Carl talk that way.'

'Have you got an Indian girl, Nickie?' Joe asked.

'No.'

'He has too, Pa,' Frank said. 'Prudence Mitchell's his girl.'

'She's not.'

'He goes to see her every day.'

'I don't.' Nick, sitting between the two boys in the dark, felt hollow and happy inside himself to be teased about Prudence Mitchell. 'She ain't my girl,' he said.

'Listen to him,' said Carl. 'I see them together every day.

'Carl can't get a girl,' his mother said, 'not even a squaw.'

Carl was quiet.

'Carl ain't no good with girls,' Frank said.

'You shut up.'

'You're all right, Carl,' Joe Garner said. 'Girls never got a man anywhere. Look at your pa.'

'Yes, that's what you would say.' Mrs Garner moved close to Joe as the waggon jolted. 'Well, you had plenty of girls in your time.'

'I'll bet pa wouldn't ever have had a squaw for a girl.'

'Don't you think it,' Joe said. 'You better watch out to keep Prudie, Nick.'

His wife whispered to him and Joe laughed.

'What you laughing at?' asked Frank.

'Don't you say it, Garner,' his wife warned. Joe laughed again.

'Nickie can have Prudence,' Joe Garner said. 'I got a good girl.'

'That the way to talk,' Mrs Garner said.

The horses were pulling heavily in the sand. Joe reached out in the dark with the whip.

'Come on, pull into it. You'll have to pull harder than this tomorrow.'

They trotted down the long hill, the waggon jolting. At the farmhouse everybody got down. Mrs Garner unlocked the door, went inside, and came out with a lamp in her hand. Carl and Nick unloaded the things from the back of the waggon. Frank sat on the front seat to drive to the barn and put up the horses. Nick went up the steps and opened the kitchen door. Mrs Garner was building a fire in the stove. She turned from pouring kerosene on the wood.

'Goodbye, Mrs Garner,' Nick said. 'Thanks for taking me.'

'Oh shucks, Nickie.'

'I had a wonderful time.'

'We like to have you. Won't you stay and eat some supper?'

'I better go. I think Dad probably waited for me.'

'Well, get along then. Send Carl up to the house, will you?'

'All right.'

'Goodnight, Nickie.'

'Goodnight, Mrs Garner.'

Nick went out the farmyard and down to the barn. Joe and Frank were milking.

'Goodnight,' Nick said. 'I had a swell time.'

'Goodnight, Nick,' Joe Garner called. 'Aren't you going to stay and eat?'

'No, I can't. Will you tell Carl his mother wants him?'

'All right. Goodnight, Nickie.'

Nick walked barefooted along the path through the meadow below the barn. The path was smooth and the dew was cool on his bare feet. He climbed a fence at the end of the meadow, went down through a ravine, his feet wet in the swamp mud, and then climbed up through the dry beech woods until he saw the lights of the cottage. He climbed over the fence and walked around to the front porch. Through the window he saw his father sitting by the table, reading in the light from the big lamp. Nick opened the door and went in.

'Well, Nickie,' his father said, 'was it a good day?'

'I had a swell time, Dad. It was a swell Fourth of July.'

'Are you hungry?'

'You bet.'

'What did you do with your shoes?'

'I left them in the waggon at Garner's.'

'Come on out to the kitchen.'

Nick's father went ahead with the lamp. He stopped and lifted the lid of the ice-box. Nick went on into the kitchen. His father brought in a piece of cold chicken on a plate and a pitcher of milk, and put them on the table before Nick. He put down the lamp.

'There's some pie too,' he said. 'Will that hold you?'

'It's grand.'

His father sat down in a chair beside the oilcloth-covered table. He made a big shadow on the kitchen wall.

'Who won the ball game?'

'Petoskey. Five to three.'

His father sat watching him eat and filled his glass from the milk-pitcher. Nick drank and wiped his mouth on his napkin. His father reached over to the shelf for the pie. He cut Nick a big piece. It was huckleberry pie.

'What did you do, Dad?'

'I went out fishing in the morning.'

'What did you get?'

'Only perch.'

His father sat watching Nick eat the pie.

'What did you do this afternoon?' Nick asked.

'I went for a walk up by the Indian camp.'

'Did you see anybody?'

'The Indians were all in town getting drunk.'

'Didn't you see anybody at all?'

'I saw your friend, Prudie.'

'Where was she?'

'She was in the woods with Frank Washburn. I ran onto them. They were having quite a time.'

His father was not looking at him.

'What were they doing?'

'I didn't stay to find out.'

'Tell me what they were doing.'

'I don't know,' his father said. 'I just heard them threshing around.'

'How did you know it was them?'

'I saw them.'

'I thought you said you didn't see them!'

'Oh, yes, I saw them.'

'Who was it with her?' Nick asked.

'Frank Washburn.'

'Were they – were they –'

'Were they what?'

'Were they happy?'

'I guess so.'

His father got up from the table and went out of the kitchen screen door. When he came back Nick was looking at his plate. He had been crying.

'Have some more?' His father picked up the knife to cut the pie.

'No,' said Nick.

'You better have another piece.'

'No, I don't want any.'

His father cleared off the table.

'Where were they in the woods?' Nick asked.

'Up back of the camp.' Nick looked at his plate. His father said. 'You better go to bed, Nick.'

'All right.'

Nick went into his room, undressed, and got into bed. He heard his father moving around in the living-room. Nick lay in the bed with his face in the pillow.

'My heart's broken,' he thought. 'If I feel this way my heart must be broken.'

After a while he heard his father blow out the lamp and go into his own room. He heard a wind come up in the trees outside and felt it come in cool through the screen. He lay for a long time with his face in the pillow, and after a while he forgot to think about Prudence and finally he went to sleep. When he awoke in the night he heard the wind in the hemlock trees outside the cottage and the waves of the lake coming in on the shore, and he went back to sleep. In the morning there was a big wind blowing and the waves were running high up on the beach and he was awake a long time before he remembered that his heart was broken.

A CANARY FOR ONE

The train passed very quickly a long, red stone house with a garden and four thick palm trees with tables under them in the shade. On the other side was the sea. Then there was a cutting through red stone and clay, and the sea was only occasionally and far below against rocks.

'I bought him in Palermo,' the American lady said. 'We only had an hour ashore and it was Sunday morning. The man wanted to be paid in dollars and I gave him a dollar and a half. He really sings very beautifully.'

It was very hot in the train and it was very hot in the *lit salon* compartment. There was no breeze came through the open window. The American lady pulled the window-blind down and there was no more sea, even occasionally. On the other side there was glass, then the corridor, then an open window, and outside the window were dusty trees and an oiled road and flat fields of grapes, with grey-stone hills behind them.

There was smoke from many tall chimneys – coming into Marseilles, and the train slowed down and followed one track through many others into the station. The train stayed twenty-five minutes in the station at Marseilles and the American lady bought a copy of the *Daily Mail* and a half-bottle of Evian water. She walked a little way along the station platform, but she stayed near the steps of the car because at Cannes, where it stopped for twelve minutes, the train had left with no signal of departure and she had only gotten on just in time. The American lady was a little deaf and she was afraid that perhaps signals of departure were given and that she did not hear them.

The train left the station in Marseilles and there was not only the switch-yards and the factory smoke but, looking back, the town of Marseilles and the harbour with stone hills behind it and the last of the sun on the water. As it was getting dark the train passed a farmhouse burning in a field. Motor-cars were stopped along the road and bedding and things from inside the farmhouse were spread in the field. Many people were watching the house burn. After it was dark the train was in Avignon. People got on and off. At the news-stand Frenchmen, returning to Paris, bought that day's French papers. On the station platforms were Negro soldiers. They wore brown uniforms and were tall and their faces shone, close under the electric light. Their faces were very black and they were too tall to stare. The train left Avignon station with the Negroes standing there. A short white sergeant was with them.

Inside the *lit salon* compartment the porter had pulled down the three beds from inside the wall and prepared them for sleeping. In the night the American lady lay without sleeping because the train was a *rapide* and went very fast and she was afraid of the speed in the night. The American lady's bed was the one next to the window. The canary from Palermo, a cloth spread over his cage, was out of the draught in the corridor that went into the compartment washroom. There was a blue light outside the compartment, and all night the train went very fast and the American lady lay awake and waited for a wreck.

In the morning the train was near Paris, and after the American lady had come out from the wash-room, looking very wholesome and middle aged and American in spite of not having slept, and had taken the cloth off the bird-cage and hung the cage in the sun, she went back to the restaurant-car for breakfast. When she came back to the *lit salon* compartment again, the beds had been pushed back into the wall and made into seats, the canary was shaking his feathers in the sunlight that came through the open window, and the train was much nearer Paris.

'He loves the sun,' the American lady said. 'He'll sing now in a little while.'

The canary shook his feathers and pecked in them. 'I've always loved birds,' the American lady said. 'I'm taking him home to my little girl. There – he's singing now.'

The canary chirped and the feathers on his throat stood out, then he dropped his bill and pecked into his feathers again. The train crossed a river and passed through a very carefully tended forest. The train passed through many outside of Paris towns. There were tram-cars in the towns and big advertisements for the Belle Jardinière and Dubonnet and Pernod on the walls towards the train. All that the train passed through looked as though it were before breakfast. For several minutes I had not listened to the American lady, who was talking to my wife.

'Is your husband American too?' asked the lady.

'Yes,' said my wife. 'We're both Americans.'

'I thought you were English.'

'Oh, no.'

'Perhaps that was because I wore braces,' I said. I had started to say suspenders and changed it to braces in the mouth, to keep my English character. The American lady did not hear. She was really quite deaf; she read lips, and I had not looked towards her. I had looked out of the window. She went on talking to my wife.

'I'm so glad you're Americans. American men make the best husbands,' the American lady was saying. 'That was why we left the Continent, you know. My daughter fell in love with a man in Vevey.' She stopped. 'They were simply madly in love.' She stopped again. 'I took her away, of course.'

'Did she get over it?' asked my wife.

'I don't think so,' said the American lady. 'She wouldn't eat anything and she wouldn't sleep at all. I've tried so very hard, but she doesn't seem to take an interest in anything. She doesn't care about things. I couldn't have her marrying a foreigner.' She paused. 'Someone, a very good friend, told me once, "No foreigner can make an American girl a good husband."'

'No,' said my wife, 'I suppose not.'

The American lady admired my wife's travelling-coat, and it turned out that the American lady had bought her own clothes for twenty years now from the same maison de couture in the rue Saint Honoré. They had her measurements, and a vendeuse who knew her and her tastes picked the dresses out for her and they were sent to America. They came to the post office near where she lived up-town in New York, and the duty was never exorbitant because they opened the dresses there in the post office to appraise them and they were always very simple-looking and with no gold lace nor ornaments that would make the dresses look expensive. Before the present vendeuse, named Thérèse, there had been another vendeuse, named Amélie. Altogether there had only been these two in the twenty years. It had always been the same couturier. Prices, however, had gone up. The exchange, though, equalized that. They had her daughter's measurements now too. She was grown up and there was not much chance of their changing now.

The train was now coming into Paris. The fortifications were levelled but grass had not grown. There were many cars standing on tracks – brown wooden restaurant-cars and brown wooden sleeping-cars that would go to Italy at five o'clock that night, if that train still left at five; the cars were marked Paris–Rome, and cars, with seats on the roofs, that went back and forth to the suburbs with, at certain hours, people in all the seats and on the roofs, if that were the way it were still done, and passing were the white walls and many windows of houses. Nothing had eaten any breakfast.

'Americans make the best husbands,' the American lady said to my wife. I was getting down the bags. 'American men are the only men in the world to marry.'

'How long ago did you leave Vevey?' asked my wife.

'Two years ago this fall. It's her, you know, that I'm taking the canary to.'

'Was the man your daughter was in love with a Swiss?'

'Yes,' said the American lady. 'He was from a very good family in Vevey. He was going to be an engineer. They met there in Vevey. They used to go on long walks together.'

'I know Vevey,' said my wife. 'We were there on our honeymoon.'

'Were you really? That must have been lovely. I had no idea, of course, that she'd fall in love with him.'

'It was a very lovely place,' said my wife.

'Yes,' said the American lady. 'Isn't it lovely? Where did you stop there?'

'We stayed at the Trois Couronnes,' said my wife.

'It's such a fine old hotel,' said the American lady.

'Yes,' said my wife. 'We had a very fine room and in the fall the country was lovely.'

'Were you there in the fall?'

'Yes,' said my wife.

We were passing three cars that had been in a wreck. They were splintered open and the roofs sagged in.

'Look,' I said. 'There's been a wreck.'

The American lady looked and saw the last car. 'I was afraid of just that all night,' she said. 'I have terrific presentiments about things sometimes. I'll never travel on a *rapide* again at night. There must be other comfortable trains that don't go so fast.'

The train was in the dark of the Gare de Lyons, and then stopped and porters came up to the windows. I handed bags through the windows, and we were out on the dim longness of the platform, and the American lady put herself in charge of one of three men from Cook's who said: 'Just a moment, madame, and I'll look for your name.'

The porter brought a truck and piled on the baggage, and my wife said good-bye and I said good-bye to the American lady whose name had been found by the man from Cook's on a typewritten page in a sheaf of typewritten pages which he replaced in his pocket.

We followed the porter with the truck down the long cement platform beside the train. At the end was a gate and a man took the tickets.

We were returning to Paris to set up separate residences.

AN ALPINE IDYLL

It was hot coming down into the valley even in the early morning. The sun melted the snow from the skis we were carrying and dried the wood. It was spring in the valley but the sun was very hot. We came along the road into Galtur carrying our skis and rucksacks. As we passed the churchyard a burial was just over. I said, 'Grüss Gott,' to the priest as he walked past us coming out of the churchyard. The priest bowed.

'It's funny a priest never speaks to you,' John said.

'You'd think they'd like to say "Grüss Gott".'

'They never answer,' John said.

We stopped in the road and watched the sexton shovelling in the new earth. A peasant with a black beard and high leather boots stood beside the grave. The sexton stopped shovelling and straightened his back. The peasant in the high boots took the spade from the sexton and went on filling in the grave – spreading the earth evenly as a man spreading manure in a garden. In the bright May morning the grave-filling looked unreal. I could not imagine anyone being dead.

'Imagine being buried on a day like this,' I said to John.

'I wouldn't like it.'

'Well,' I said, 'we don't have to do it.'

We went on up the road past the houses of the town to the inn. We had been skiing in the Silvretta for a month, and it was good to be down in the valley. In the Silvretta the skiing had been all right, but it was spring skiing, the snow was good only in the early morning and again in the evening. The rest of the time it was spoiled by the sun. We were both tired of the sun. You could not get away from the sun. The only shadows were made by rocks or by the hut that was built under the protection of a rock beside a glacier, and in the shade the sweat froze in your underclothing. You could not sit outside the hut without dark glasses. It was pleasant to be burned black but the sun had been very tiring. You could not rest in it. I was glad to be down away from snow. It was too late in the spring to be up in the Silvretta. I was a little tired of skiing. We had stayed too long. I could taste the snow water we had been drinking melted off the tin roof of the hut. The taste was a part of the way I felt about skiing. I was glad there were other things beside skiing, and I was glad to be down, away from the unnatural high mountain spring, into this May morning in the valley.

The innkeeper sat on the porch of the inn his chair tipped back against the wall. Beside him sat the cook.

'Ski-heil!' said the innkeeper.

'Heil!' we said and leaned the skis against the wall and took off our packs.

'How was it up above?' asked the innkeeper.

'Schön. A little too much sun.'

'Yes. There's too much sun this time of year.'

The cook sat on in his chair. The innkeeper went in with us and unlocked his office and brought out our mail. There was a bundle of letters and some papers.

'Let's get some beer,' John said.

'Good. We'll drink it inside.'

The proprietor brought two bottles and we drank them while we read the letters.

'We better have some more beer,' John said. A girl brought it this time. She smiled as she opened the bottles.

'Many letters,' she said.

'Yes. Many.'

'Prosit,' she said and went out, taking the empty bottles.

'I'd forgotten what beer tasted like.'

'I hadn't,' John said. 'Up in the hut I used to think about it a lot.'

'Well,' I said, 'we've got it now.'

'You oughtn't to ever do anything too long.'

'No. We were up there too long.'

'Too damn long,' John said. 'It's no good doing a thing too long.'

The sun came through the open window and shone through the beer bottles on the table. The bottles were half full. There was a little froth on the beer in the bottles, not much, because it was very cold. It collared up when you poured it into the tall glasses. I looked out of the open window at the white road. The trees beside the road were dusty. Beyond was a green field and a stream. There were trees along the stream and a mill with a water wheel. Through the open side of the mill I saw a long log and a saw in it rising and falling. No one seemed to be tending it. There were four crows walking in the green field. One crow sat in a tree watching. Outside on the porch the cook got off his chair and passed into the hall that led back into the kitchen. Inside, the sunlight shone through the empty glasses on the table. John was leaning forward with his head on his arms.

Through the window I saw two men come up the front steps. They came into the drinking room. One was the bearded peasant in the high boots. The other was the sexton. They sat down at the table under the window. The girl came in and stood by their table. The peasant did not seem to see her. He sat with his hands on the table. He wore his old army clothes. There were patches on the elbows.

'What will it be?' asked the sexton. The peasant did not pay any attention.

'What will you drink?'

'Schnapps,' the peasant said.

'And a quarter litre of red wine,' the sexton told the girl.

The girl brought the drinks and the peasant drank the schnapps. He looked out of the window. The sexton watched him. John had his head forward on the table. He was asleep.

The innkeeper came in and went over to the table. He spoke in dialect and the sexton answered him. The peasant looked out of the window. The innkeeper went out of the room. The peasant stood up. He took a folded ten-thousand kronen note out of a leather pocketbook and unfolded it. The girl came up.

'Alles?' she asked.

'Alles,' he said.

'Let me buy the wine,' the sexton said.

'Alles,' the peasant repeated to the girl. She put her hand in the pocket of her apron, brought it out full of coins and counted out the change. The peasant went out of the door. As soon as he was gone the innkeeper came into the room again and spoke to the sexton. He sat down at the table. They talked in dialect. The sexton was amused. The innkeeper was disgusted. The sexton stood up from the table. He was a little man with a moustache. He leaned out of the window and looked up the road.

'There he goes in,' he said.

'In the Löwen?'

'Ja.'

They talked again and then the innkeeper came over to our table. The innkeeper was a tall man and old. He looked at John asleep.

'He's pretty tired.'

'Yes, we were up early.'

'Will you want to eat soon?'

'Any time,' I said. 'What is there to eat?'

'Anything you want. The girl will bring the eating-card.'

The girl brought the menu. John woke up. The menu was written in ink on a card and the card slipped into a wooden paddle.

'There's the Speisekarte,' I said to John. He looked at it. He was still sleepy.

'Won't you have a drink with us?' I asked the innkeeper. He sat down. 'Those peasants are beasts,' said the innkeeper.

'We saw that one at a funeral coming into town.'

'That was his wife.'

'Oh.'

'He's a beast. All these peasants are beasts.'

'How do you mean?'

'You wouldn't believe it. You wouldn't believe what just happened about that one.'

'Tell me.'

'You wouldn't believe it.' The innkeeper spoke to the sexton. 'Franz, come over here.' The sexton came, bringing his little bottle of wine and his glass.

'The gentlemen are just come down from the Wiesbadener-hütte,' the innkeeper said. We shook hands.

'What will you drink?' I asked.

'Nothing,' Franz shook his finger.

'Another quarter litre?'

'All right.'

'Do you understand dialect?' the innkeeper asked.

'No.'

'What's it all about?' John asked.

'He's going to tell us about the peasant we saw filling the grave, coming into town.'

'I can't understand it, anyway,' John said. 'It goes too fast for me.'

'That peasant,' the innkeeper said, 'today he brought his wife in to be buried. She died last November.'

'December,' said the sexton.

'That makes nothing. She died last December then, and he notified the commune.'

'December eighteenth,' said the sexton.

'Anyway, he couldn't bring her over to be buried until the snow was gone.'

'He lives on the other side of the Paznaun,' said the sexton. 'But he belongs to this parish.'

'He couldn't bring her out at all?' I asked.

'No. He can only come, from where he lives, on skis until the snow melts. So today he brought her in to be buried and the priest, when he looked at her face, didn't want to bury her. You go on and tell it,' he said to the sexton. 'Speak German, not dialect.'

'It was very funny with the priest,' said the sexton. 'In the report to the commune she died of heart trouble. We knew she had heart trouble here. She used to faint in church sometimes. She did not come for a long time. She wasn't strong to climb. When the priest uncovered her face he asked Olz, "Did your wife suffer much?" "No," said Olz. "When I came in the house she was dead across the bed."'

'The priest looked at her again. He didn't like it.

' "How did her face get that way?"

' "I don't know,' Olz said.

' "You'd better find out," the priest said, and put the blanket back. Olz didn't say anything. The priest looked at him. Olz looked back at the priest. "You want to know?"

' "I must know," the priest said.'

'This is where it's good,' the innkeeper said. 'Listen to this. Go on, Franz.'

' "Well," said Olz, "when she died I made the report to the commune and I put her in the shed across the top of the big wood. When I started to use the big wood she was stiff and I put her up against the wall. Her mouth was open and when I came into the shed at night to cut up the big wood, I hung the lantern from it."

' "Why did you do that?" asked the priest.

' "I don't know," said Olz.

' "Did you do that many times?"

' "Every time I went to work in the shed at night."

' "It was very wrong," said the priest. "Did you love your wife?"

' "Ja, I loved her," Olz said. "I loved her fine."

'Did you understand it all?' asked the innkeeper. 'You understand it all about his wife?'

'I heard it.'

'How about eating?' John asked.

'You order,' I said. 'Do you think it's true?' I asked the innkeeper.

'Sure it's true,' he said. 'These peasants are beasts.'

'Where did he go now?'

'He's gone to drink at my colleague's, the Löwen.'

'He didn't want to drink with me,' said the sexton.

'He didn't want to drink with him, after he knew about his wife,' said the innkeeper.

'Say,' said John. 'How about eating?'

'All right,' I said.

A PURSUIT RACE

William Campbell had been in a pursuit race with a burlesque show ever since Pittsburgh. In a pursuit race, in bicycle racing, riders start at equal intervals to ride after one another. They ride very fast because the race is usually limited to a short distance and if they slow their riding another rider who maintains his pace will make up the space that separated them equally at the start. As soon as a rider is caught and passed he is out of the race and must get down from his bicycle and leave the track. If none of the riders are caught the winner of the race is the one who has gained the most distance. In most pursuit races, if there are only two riders, one of the riders is caught inside of six miles. The burlesque show caught William Campbell at Kansas City.

William Campbell had hoped to hold a slight lead over the burlesque show until they reached the Pacific coast. As long as he preceded the burlesque show as advance man he was being paid. When the burlesque show caught up with him he was in bed. He was in bed when the manager of the burlesque troupe came into his room and after the manager had gone out he decided that he might as well stay in bed. It was very cold in Kansas City and he was in no hurry to go out. He did not like Kansas City. He reached under the bed for a bottle and drank. It made his stomach feel better. Mr Turner, the manager of the burlesque show, had refused a drink.

William Campbell's interview with Mr Turner had been a little strange. Mr Turner had knocked on the door. Campbell had said: 'Come in!' When Mr Turner came into the room he saw clothing on a chair, an open suitcase, the bottle on a chair beside the bed, and someone lying in the bed completely covered by the bed-clothes.

'Mister Campbell,' Mr Turner said.

'You can't fire me,' William Campbell said from underneath the covers. It was warm and white and close under the covers. 'You can't fire me because I've got down off my bicycle.'

'You're drunk,' Mr Turner said.

'Oh, yes,' William Campbell said, speaking directly against the sheet and feeling the texture with his lips.

'You're a fool,' Mr Turner said. He turned off the electric light. The electric light had been burning all night. It was now ten o'clock in the morning. 'You're a drunken fool. When did you get into this town?'

'I got into this town last night,' William Campbell said, speaking against the sheet. He found he liked to talk through a sheet. 'Did you ever talk through a sheet?'

'Don't try to be funny. You aren't funny.'

'I'm not being funny. I'm just talking through a sheet.'

'You're talking through a sheet all right.'

'You can go now, Mr Turner,' Campbell said. 'I don't work for you any more.'

'You know that anyway.'

'I know a lot,' William Campbell said. He pulled down the sheet and looked at Mr Turner. 'I know enough so I don't mind looking at you at all. Do you want to hear what I know?'

'No.'

'Good,' said William Campbell. 'Because really I don't know anything at all. I was just talking.' He pulled the sheet up over his face again. 'I love it under a sheet,' he said. Mr Turner stood beside the bed. He was a middle-aged man with a large stomach and a bald head and he had many things to do. 'You ought to stop off here, Billy, and take a cure,' he said. 'I'll fix it up if you want to do it.'

'I don't want to take a cure,' William Campbell said. 'I don't want to take a cure at all. I am perfectly happy. All my life I have been perfectly happy.'

'How long have you been this way?'

'What a question!' William Campbell breathed in and out through the sheet.

'How long have you been stewed, Billy?'

'Haven't I done my work?'

'Sure. I just asked you how long you've been stewed, Billy.'

'I don't know. But I've got my wolf back,' he touched the sheet with his tongue. 'I've had him for a week.'

'The hell you have.'

'Oh, yes. My dear wolf. Every time I take a drink he goes outside the room. He can't stand alcohol. The poor little fellow.' He moved his tongue round and round on the sheet. 'He's a lovely wolf. He's just like he always was.' William Campbell shut his eyes and took a deep breath.

'You got to take a cure, Billy,' Mr Turner said. 'You won't mind the Keeley. It isn't bad.'

'The Keeley,' William Campbell said. 'It isn't far from London.' He shut his eyes and opened them, moving the eyelashes against the sheet. 'I just love sheets,' he said. He looked at Mr Turner.

'Listen, you think I'm drunk.'

'You *are* drunk.'

'No, I'm not.'

'You're drunk and you've had dt's.'

'No.' William Campbell held the sheet around his head. 'Dear sheet,' he said. He breathed against it gently. 'Pretty sheet. You love me, don't you, sheet? It's all in the price of the room. Just like in Japan. No,' he said. 'Listen Billy, dear Sliding Billy, I have a surprise for you. I'm not drunk. I'm hopped to the eyes.'

'No,' said Mr Turner.

'Take a look.' William Campbell pulled up the right sleeve of his pyjama jacket under the sheet, then shoved the right forearm out. 'Look at that.' On the forearm, from just above the wrist to the elbow, were small blue circles around tiny dark blue punctures. The circles almost touched one another. 'That's the new development,' William Campbell said. 'I drink a little now once in awhile, just to drive the wolf out of the room.'

'They got a cure for that,' 'Sliding Billy' Turner said.

'No,' William Campbell said. 'They haven't got a cure for anything.'

'You can't just quit like that, Billy,' Turner said. He sat on the bed.

'Be careful of my sheet,' William Campbell said.

116

'You can't just quit at your age and take to pumping your-self full of that stuff just because you got in a jam.'

'There's a law against it. If that's what you mean.'

'No, I mean you got to fight it out.'

Billy Campbell caressed the sheet with his lips and his tongue. 'Dear sheet,' he said. 'I can kiss this sheet and see right through it at the same time.'

'Cut it out about the sheet. You can't just take to that stuff, Billy.'

William Campbell shut his eyes. He was beginning to feel a slight nausea. He knew that this nausea would increase steadily, without there ever being the relief of sickness, until something were done against it. It was at this point that he suggested that Mr Turner have a drink. Mr Turner declined. William Campbell took a drink from the bottle. It was a temporary measure. Mr Turner watched him. Mr Turner had been in this room much longer than he should have been, he had many things to do; although living in daily association with people who used drugs, he had a horror of drugs, and he was very fond of William Campbell; he did not wish to leave him. He was very sorry for him and he felt a cure might help. He knew there were good cures in Kansas City. But he had to go. He stood up.

'Listen, Billy,' William Campbell said, 'I want to tell you something. You're called "Sliding Billy". That's because you can slide. I'm called just Billy. That's because I never could slide at all. I can't slide, Billy. I can't slide. It just catches. Every time I try it, it catches.' He shut his eyes. 'I can't slide, Billy. It's awful when you can't slide.'

'Yes,' said 'Sliding Billy' Turner.

'Yes, what?' William Campbell looked at him.

'You were saying.'

'No,' said William Campbell. 'I wasn't saying. It must have been a mistake.'

'You were saying about sliding.'

'No. It couldn't have been about sliding. But listen, Billy, and I'll tell you a secret. Stick to sheets, Billy. Keep away from women and horses and, and –' he stopped '– eagles, Billy. If you love horses you'll get horse-s –, and if you love eagles you'll get eagle-s –.' He stopped and put his head under the sheet.

'I got to go,' said 'Sliding Billy' Turner.

'If you love women you'll get a dose,' William Campbell said. 'If you love horses –'

'Yes, you said that.'

'Said what?'

'About horses and eagles.'

'Oh, yes. And if you love sheets.' He breathed on the sheet and stroked his nose against it. 'I don't know about sheets,' he said. 'I just started to love this sheet.'

'I have to go,' Mr Turner said. 'I got a lot to do.'

'That's all right,' William Campbell said. 'Everybody's got to go.'

'I better go.'

'All right, you go.'

'Are you all right, Billy?'

'I was never so happy in my life.'

'And you're all right?'

'I'm fine. You go along. I'll just lie here for a little while. Around noon I'll get up.'

But when Mr Turner came up to William Campbell's room at noon William Campbell was sleeping and as Mr Turner was a man who knew what things in life were very valuable he did not wake him.

TODAY IS FRIDAY

Three Roman soldiers are in a drinking-place at eleven o'clock at night. There are barrels around the wall. Behind the wooden counter is a Hebrew wine-seller. The three Roman soldiers are a little cock-eyed.

1st Roman Soldier – You tried the red?

2nd Soldier – No, I ain't tried it.

1st Soldier – You better try it.

2nd Soldier – All right, George, we'll have a round of the red.

Hebrew Wine-seller – Here you are, gentlemen. You'll like that. [*He sets down an earthenware pitcher that he has filled from one of the casks.*] That's a nice little wine.

1st Soldier – Have a drink of it yourself. [*He turns to the third Roman soldier who is leaning on a barrel.*] What's the matter with you?

3rd Roman Soldier – I got a gut-ache.

2nd Soldier – You've been drinking water.

1st Soldier – Try some of the red.

3rd Soldier – I can't drink the damn stuff. It makes my gut sour.

1st Soldier – You been out here too long.

3rd Soldier – Hell, don't I know it?

1st Soldier – Say, George, can't you give this gentleman something to fix up his stomach?

Hebrew Wine-seller – I got it right here.

[*The third Roman soldier tastes the cup that the wine-seller has mixed for him.*]

3rd Soldier – Hey, what you put in that, camel chips?

Wine-seller – You drink that right down, Lootenant. That'll fix you up right.

3rd Soldier – Well, I couldn't feel any worse.

1st Soldier – Take a chance on it. George fixed me up fine the other day.

Wine-seller – You were in bad shape, Lootenant. I know what fixes up a bad stomach.

[*The third Roman soldier drinks the cup down.*]

3rd Roman Soldier – Jesus Christ. [*He makes a face.*]

2nd Soldier – That false alarm!

1st Soldier – Oh, I don't know. He was pretty good in there today.

2nd Soldier – Why didn't he come down off the cross?

1st Soldier – He didn't want to come down off the cross. That's not his play.

2nd Soldier – Show me a guy that doesn't want to come down off the cross.

1st Soldier – Aw, hell, you don't know anything about it. Ask George there. Did he want to come down off the cross, George?

Wine-seller – I'll tell you, gentlemen, I wasn't out there. It's a thing I haven't taken any interest in.

2nd Soldier – Listen, I seen a lot of them – here and plenty of other places. Any time you show me one that doesn't want to get down off the cross when the time comes – when the time comes, I mean – I'll climb up with him.

1st Soldier – I thought he was pretty good in there today.

3rd Soldier – He was all right.

2nd Roman Soldier – You guys don't know what I'm talking about. I'm not saying whether he was good or not. What I mean is, when the time comes. When they first start nailing him, there isn't none of them wouldn't stop it if they could.

1st Soldier – Didn't you follow it, George?

Wine-seller – No, I didn't take any interest in it, Lootenant.

1st Soldier – I was surprised how he acted.

3rd Soldier – The part I don't like is the nailing them on. You know, that must get to you pretty bad.

2nd Soldier – It isn't that that's so bad, as when they first lift 'em. [*He makes a lifting gesture with his two palms together.*] When the weight starts to pull on 'em. That's when it gets 'em.

3rd Roman Soldier – It takes some of them pretty bad.

1st Soldier – Ain't I seen 'em? I seen plenty of them. I tell you, he was pretty good in there today.

[*The second Roman soldier smiles at the Hebrew wine-seller.*]

2nd Soldier – You're a regular Christer, big boy.

1st Soldier – Sure, go on and kid him. But listen while I tell you something. He was pretty good in there today.

2nd Soldier – What about some more wine?

[*The wine-seller looks up expectantly. The third Roman soldier is sitting with his head down. He does not look well.*]

3rd Soldier – I don't want any more.

2nd Soldier – –Just for two, George.

[*The wine-seller puts out a pitcher of wine, a size smaller than the last one. He leans forward on the wooden counter.*]

1st Roman Soldier – You see his girl?

2nd Soldier – Wasn't I standing right by her?

1st Soldier – She's a nice looker.

2nd Soldier – I knew her before he did. [*He winks at the wine-seller.*]

1st Soldier – I used to see her around the town.

2nd Soldier – She used to have a lot of stuff. He never brought *her* no good luck.

1st Soldier – Oh, he ain't lucky. But he looked pretty good to me in there today.

2nd Soldier – What became of his gang?

1st Soldier – Oh, they faded out. Just the women stuck by him.

2nd Roman Soldier – They were a pretty yellow crowd. When they seen him go up there they didn't want any of it.

1st Soldier – The women stuck all right.

2nd Soldier – Sure, they stuck all right.

1st Roman Soldier – You see me slip the old spear into him?

2nd Roman Soldier – You'll get into trouble doing that some day.

1st Soldier – It was the least I could do for him. I'll tell you he looked pretty good to me in there today.

Hebrew wine-seller – Gentlemen, you know I got to close.

1st Roman Soldier – We'll have one more round.

2nd Roman Soldier – What's the use? This stuff don't get you anywhere. Come on, let's go.

1st Soldier – Just another round.

3rd Roman Soldier – [*Getting up from the barrel.*] No, come on. Let's go. I feel like hell tonight.

1st Soldier – Just one more.

2nd Soldier – No, come on. We're going to go. Goodnight, George. Put it on the bill.

Wine-seller – Goodnight, gentlemen. [*He looks a little worried.*] You couldn't let me have a little something on account, Lootenant?

2nd Roman Soldier – What the hell, George! Wednesday's payday.

Wine-seller – It's all right, Lootenant. Goodnight, gentlemen.

[*The three Roman soldiers go out the door into the street.*]

[*Outside in the street.*]

2nd Roman Soldier – George is a kike just like all the rest of them.

1st Roman Soldier – Oh, George is a nice fella.

2nd Soldier – Everybody's a nice fella to you tonight.

3rd Roman Soldier – Come on, let's go up to the barracks. I feel like hell tonight.

2nd Soldier – You been out here too long.

3rd Roman Soldier – No, it ain't just that. I feel like hell.

2nd Soldier – You been out here too long. That's all.

CURTAIN.

So he ate an orange, slowly spitting out the seeds. Outside, the snow was turning to rain. Inside, the electric stove seemed to give no heat and rising from his writing-table, he sat down upon the stove. How good it felt! Here, at last, was life.

He reached for another orange. Far away in Paris, Mascart had knocked Danny Frush cuckoo in the second round. Far off in Mesopotamia, twenty-one feet of snow had fallen. Across the world in distant Australia, the English cricketers were sharpening up their wickets. *There* was Romance.

Patrons of the arts and letters have discovered *The Forum*, he read. It is the guide, philosopher, and friend of the thinking minority. Prize short-stories – will their authors write our best-sellers of tomorrow?

You will enjoy these warm, homespun, American tales, bits of real life on the open ranch, in crowded tenement or comfortable home, and all with a healthy undercurrent of humour.

I must read them, he thought.

He read on. Our children's children – what of them? Who of them? New means must be discovered to find room for us under the sun. Shall this be done by war or can it be done by peaceful methods?

Or will we all have to move to Canada?

Our deepest convictions – will Science upset them? Our civilization – is it inferior to older orders of things?

And meanwhile, in the far-off dripping jungles of Yucatán, sounded the chopping of the axes of the gum-choppers.

Do we want big men – or do we want them cultured? Take Joyce. Take President Coolidge. What star must our college students aim at? There is Jack Britton. There is Dr Henry Van Dyke. Can we reconcile the two? Take the case of Young Stribling.

And what of our daughters who must make their own Soundings? Nancy Hawthorne is obliged to make her own Soundings in the sea of life. Bravely and sensibly she faces the problems which come to every girl of eighteen.

It was a splendid booklet.

Are you a girl of eighteen? Take the case of a Joan of Arc. Take the case of Bernard Shaw. Take the case of Betsy Ross.

Think of these things in 1925 – Was there a risqué page in Puritan history? Were there two sides to Pocahontas? Did she have a fourth dimension?

Are modern paintings – and poetry – Art? Yes and No. Take Picasso.

Have tramps codes of conduct? Send your mind adventuring.

There is Romance everywhere. *Forum* writers talk to the point, are possessed of humour and wit. But they do not try to be smart and are never long-winded.

Live the full life of the mind, exhilarated by new ideas, intoxicated by the Romance of the unusual. He laid down the booklet.

And meanwhile, stretched flat on a bed in a darkened room in the house in Triana, Manuel Garcia Maera lay with a tube in each lung, drowning with the penumonia. All the papers in Andalucia devoted special supplements to his death, which had been expected for some days. Men and boys bought full-length coloured pictures of him to remember him by, and lost the picture they had of him in their memories by looking at the lithographs. Bullfighters were very relieved he was dead, because he did always in the bullring the things they could only do sometimes. They all marched in the rain behind his coffin and there were one hundred and forty-seven bull-fighters followed him out to the cemetery where they buried him in the tomb next to Joselito. After the funeral every one sat in the cafés out of the rain, and many coloured pictures of Maera were sold to men who rolled them up and put them away in their pockets.

NOW I LAY ME

That night we lay on the floor in the room and I listened to the silkworms eating. The silkworms fed in racks of mulberry leaves and all night you could hear them eating and a dropping sound in the leaves. I myself did not want to sleep because I had been living for a long time with the knowledge that if I ever shut my eyes in the dark and let myself go, my soul would go out of my body. I had been that way for a long time, ever since I had been blown up at night and felt it go out of me and go off and then come back. I tried never to think about it, but it had started to go since, in the nights, just at the moment of going off to sleep, and I could only stop it by a very great effort. So while now I am fairly sure that it would not really have gone out, yet then, that summer, I was unwilling to make the experiment.

I had different ways of occupying myself while I lay awake. I would think of a trout stream I had fished along when I was a boy and fish its whole length very carefully in my mind; fishing very carefully under all the logs, all the turns of the bank, the deep holes and the clear shallow stretches, sometimes catching trout and sometimes losing them. I would stop fishing at noon to eat my lunch; sometimes on a log over the stream; sometimes on a high bank under a tree, and I always ate my lunch very slowly and watched the stream below me while I ate. Often I ran out of bait because I would take only ten worms with me in a tobacco tin when I started. When I had used them all I had to find more worms, and sometimes it was very difficult digging in the bank of the stream where the cedar trees kept out the sun and there was no grass but only the bare moist earth and often I could find no worms. Always though I found some kind of bait, but one time in the swamp I could find no bait at all and had to cut up one of the trout I had caught and use him for bait.

Sometimes I found insects in the swamp meadows, in the grass or under ferns, and used them. There were beetles and insects with legs like grass stems, and grubs in old rotten logs; white grubs with brown pinching heads that would not stay on the hook and emptied into nothing in the cold water, and wood ticks under logs where sometimes I found angle-worms that slipped into the ground as soon as the log was raised. Once I used a salamander from under an old log. The salamander was very small and neat and agile and a lovely colour. He had tiny feet that tried to hold on to the hook, and after that one time I never used a salamander, although I found them very often. Nor did I use crickets, because of the way they acted about the hook.

Sometimes the stream ran through an open meadow, and in the dry grass I would catch grasshoppers and use them for bait and sometimes I would catch grasshoppers and toss them into the stream and watch them float along swimming on the stream and circling on the surface as the current took them and then disappear as a trout rose. Sometimes I would fish four or five different streams in the night; starting as near as I could get to their source and fishing them down stream. When I had finished too quickly and the time did not go, I would fish the stream over again, starting where it emptied into the lake and fishing back up stream, trying for all the trout I had missed coming down. Some nights too I made up streams, and some of them were very exciting, and it was like being awake and dreaming. Some of those streams I still remember and think that I have fished in them, and they are confused with streams I really know. I gave them all names and went to them on the train and sometimes walked for miles to get to them.

But some nights I could not fish, and on those nights I was cold-awake and said my prayers over and over and tried to pray for all the people I had ever known. That took up a great amount of time, for if you try to remember all the people you have ever known, going back to the earliest thing you remember – which was, with me, the attic of the house where I was born and my mother and father's wedding-cake in a tin box hanging from one of the rafters, and, in the attic, jars of snakes and other specimens that my father had collected as a boy and preserved in alcohol, the alcohol sunken in the jars so the backs of some of the snakes and specimens were exposed and had turned white – if you thought back that far, you remembered a great many people. If you prayed for all of them, saying a Hail Mary and Our Father for each one, it took a long time and finally it would be light, and then you could go to sleep, if you were in a place where you could sleep in the daylight.

On those nights I tried to remember everything that had ever happened to me, starting with just before I went to the war and remembering back from one thing to another. I found I could only remember back to that attic in my grandfather's house. Then I would start there and remember this way again, until I reached the war.

I remembered, after my grandfather died we moved away from that house and to a new house designed and built by my mother. Many things that were not to be moved were burned in the back-yard and I remember those jars from the attic being thrown in the fire, and how they popped in the heat and the fire flamed up from the alcohol. I remember the snakes burning in the fire in the backyard. But there were no people in that, only things. I could not remember who burned the things even, and I would go on until I came to people and then stop and pray for them.

About the new house I remembered how my mother was always cleaning things out and making a good clearance. One time when my father was away on a hunting trip she made a good thorough cleaning out in the basement and burned everything that should not have been there. When my father came home and got down from his buggy and hitched the horse, the fire was still burning in the road beside the house. I went out to meet him. He handed me his shotgun and looked at the fire. 'What's this?' he asked.

'I've been cleaning out the basement, dear,' my mother said from the porch. She was standing there smiling, to meet him. My father looked at the fire and kicked at something. Then he leaned over and picked something out of the ashes. 'Get a rake, Nick,' he said to me. I went to the basement and brought a rake and my father raked very carefully in the ashes. He raked out stone axes and stone skinning knives and tools for marking arrow-heads and pieces of pottery and many arrowheads.

They had all been blackened and chipped by the fire. My father raked them all out very carefully and spread them on the grass by the road. His shotgun in its leather case and his game-bags were on the grass where he had left them when he stepped down from the buggy.

'Take the gun and the bags in the house, Nick, and bring me a paper,' he said. My mother had gone inside the house. I took the shotgun, which was heavy to carry and banged against my legs, and the two game-bags and started towards the house. 'Take them one at a time,' my father said. 'Don't try and carry too much at once.' I put down the game-bags and took in the shotgun and brought out a newspaper from the pile in my father's office. My father spread all the blackened, chipped stone implements on the paper and then wrapped them up. 'The best arrow-heads went all to pieces,' he said. He walked into the house with the paper package and I stayed outside on the grass with the two game-bags. After a while, I took them in. In remembering that, there were only two people, so I would pray for them both.

Some nights, though, I could not remember my prayers even. I could only get as far as 'On earth as it is in heaven' and then have to start all over and be absolutely unable to get past that. Then I would have to recognize that I could not remember and give up saying my prayers that night and try something else. So on some nights I would try to remember all the animals in the world by name and then the birds and then fishes and then countries and cities and then kinds of food and the names of all the streets I could remember in Chicago, and when I could not remember anything at all any more I would just listen. And I do not remember a night on which you could not hear things. If I could have a light I was not afraid to sleep, because I knew my soul would only go out of me if it were dark. So, of course, many nights I was where I could have a light and then I slept because I was nearly always tired and often very sleepy. And I am sure many times too that I slept without knowing it – but I never slept knowing it, and on this night I listened to the silkworms. You can hear silk-worms eating very clearly in the night and I lay with my eyes open and listened to them.

There was only one other person in the room and he was awake too. I listened to him being awake, for a long time. He could not lie as quietly as I could because, perhaps, he had not had so much practice being awake. We were lying on blankets spread over straw and when he moved the straw was noisy, but the silkworms were not frightened by any noise we made and ate on steadily. There were the noises of night seven kilometres behind the lines outside but they were different from the small noises inside the room in the dark. The other man in the room tried lying quietly. Then he moved again. I moved too, so he would know I was awake. He had lived ten years in Chicago. They had taken him for a soldier in nineteen fourteen when he had come back to visit his family, and they had given him to me for an orderly because he spoke English. I heard him listening, so I moved again in the blankets.

'Can't you sleep, signor tenente?' he asked.

'No.'

'I can't sleep, either.'

'What's the matter?'

'I don't know. I can't sleep.'

'You feel all right?'

'Sure. I feel good. I just can't sleep.'

'You want to talk a while?' I asked.

'Sure. What can you talk about in this damn place.'

'This place is pretty good,' I said.

'Sure,' he said. 'It's all right.'

'Tell me about out in Chicago,' I said.

'Oh,' he said, 'I told you all that once.'

'Tell me about how you got married.'

'I told you that.'

'Was the letter you got Monday – from her?'

'Sure. She writes me all the time. She's making good money with the place.'

'You'll have a nice place when you go back.'

'Sure. She runs it fine. She's making a lot of money.'

'Don't you think we'll wake them up, talking?' I asked.

'No. They can't hear. Anyway, they sleep like pigs. I'm different,' he said. 'I'm nervous.'

'Talk quiet,' I said. 'Want a smoke?'

We smoked skilfully in the dark.

'You don't smoke much, signor tenente.'

'No. I've just about cut it out.'

'Well,' he said, 'it don't do you any good and I suppose you get so you don't miss it. Did you ever hear a blind man won't smoke because he can't see the smoke come out?'

'I don't believe it.'

'I think it's all bull, myself,' he said. 'I just heard it somewhere. You know how you hear things.'

We were both quiet and I listened to the silkworms.

'You hear those damn silkworms?' he asked. 'You can hear them chew.'

'It's funny,' I said.

'Say, signor tenente, is there something really the matter that you can't sleep? I never see you sleep. You haven't slept nights ever since I been with you.'

'I don't know, John,' I said. 'I got in pretty bad shape along early last spring and at night it bothers me.'

'Just like I am,' he said. 'I shouldn't have ever got in this war. I'm too nervous.'

'Maybe it will get better.'

'Say, signor tenente, what did you get in this war for, anyway?'

'I don't know, John. I wanted to, then.'

'Wanted to,' he said. 'That's a hell of a reason.'

'We oughtn't to talk out loud,' I said.

'They sleep just like pigs,' he said. 'They can't understand the English language, anyway. They don't know a damn thing. What are you going to do when it's over and we go back to the States?'

'I'll get a job on a paper.'

'In Chicago?'

'Maybe.'

'Do you ever read what this fellow Brisbane writes? My wife cuts it out for me and sends it to me.'

'Sure.'

'Did you ever meet him?'

'No, but I've seen him.'

'I'd like to meet that fellow. He's a fine writer. My wife

don't read English but she takes the paper just like when I was home and she cuts out the editorials and the sports page and sends them to me.'

'How are your kids?'

'They're fine. One of the girls is in the fourth grade now. You know, signor tenente, if I didn't have the kids I wouldn't be your orderly now. They'd have made me stay in the line all the time.'

'I'm glad you've got them.'

'So am I. They're fine kids but I want a boy. Three girls and no boy. That's a hell of a note.'

'Why don't you try and go to sleep.'

'No, I can't sleep now. I'm wide awake now, signor tenente. Say, I'm worried about you not sleeping, though.'

'It'll be all right, John.'

'Imagine a young fellow like you not to sleep.'

'I'll get all right. It just takes a while.'

'You got to get all right. A man can't get along that don't sleep. Do you worry about anything? You got anything on your mind?'

'No, John, I don't think so.'

'You ought to get married, signor tenente. Then you wouldn't worry.'

'I don't know.'

'You ought to get married. Why don't you pick out some nice Italian girl with plenty of money? You could get any one you want. You're young and you got good decorations and you look nice. You been wounded a couple of times.'

'I can't talk the language well enough.'

'You talk it fine. To hell with talking the language. You don't have to talk to them. Marry them.'

'I'll think about it.'

'You know some girls, don't you?'

'Sure.'

'Well, you marry the one with the most money. Over here, the way they're brought up, they'll all make you a good wife.'

'I'll think about it.'

'Don't think about it, signor tenente. Do it.'

'All right.'

'A man ought to be married. You'll never regret it. Every man ought to be married.'

'All right,' I said. 'Let's try and sleep a while.'

'All right, signor tenente. I'll try it again. But you remember what I said.'

'I'll remember it,' I said. 'Now let's sleep a while, John.'

'All right,' he said. 'I hope you sleep, signor tenente.'

I heard him roll in his blankets on the straw and then he was very quiet and I listened to him breathing regularly. Then he started to snore. I listened to him snore for a long time and then I stopped listening to him snore and listened to the silk-worms eating. They ate steadily, making a dropping in the leaves. I had a new thing to think about and I lay in the dark with my eyes open and thought of all the girls I had ever known and what kind of wives they would make. It was a very interesting thing to think about and for a while it killed off trout-fishing and interfered with my prayers. Finally, though, I went back to trout-fishing, because I found that I could remember all the streams and there was always something new about them, while the girls, after I had thought about them a few times, blurred and I could not call them into my mind and finally they all blurred and all became rather the same and I gave up thinking about them almost altogether. But I kept on with my prayers and I prayed very often for John in the nights and his class was removed from active service before the October offensive. I was glad he was not there, because he would have been a great worry to me. He came to the hospital in Milan to see me several months after and was very disappointed that I had not yet married, and I know he would feel very badly if he knew that, so far, I have never married. He was going back to America and he was very certain about marriage and knew it would fix up everything.